The Midget Green Swamp Moose

Keith Lawrence Roman

Morningside Books

Morningside Books Trade Paperback Edition

Copyright © 2010 Keith Lawrence Roman

All rights reserved.
Published in the United States of America by
Morningside Books, Orlando, Florida

This edition is cataloged as:
ISBN 978-0-9827288-0-2

www.Morningsidebooks.net

Printed in the United States of America

For Skippy and Pokey

Acknowledgement:

A special thank you to my sixth grade teacher, Phillip A. Shart, then just around thirty years old, who taught me to believe that anyone can do great things, even if they are only 12 years old.

K. L. R.

Prologue

Did you ever try not to laugh at something and the more you try not to, the harder it is to stop? Next thing you know you're laughin' and guffawin' so much you can't hardly stand it. Your stomach tightens up and tears stream out of your eyes. If you're sitting on a chair you fall right off. You swallow little gulps of air trying to settle yourself but it really doesn't help. You just laugh and laugh and hold onto your middle trying to keep your ribs from hurting.

That's what happened to my brother Bret and me. We had been feeling lower than the belly button on a short toad when we got caught up in a round of giggling I thought would never end. Of course it did, otherwise I wouldn't be able to tell you our story. I'd still be rolling around on the ground, covered in pond slime, laughin' at next to nothin'.

Chapter One

The old iron schoolbell clanged endlessly while our teacher, Miss Crisp, kept prattling on about seeing us in September and how we should have a good summer and the like. Truthfully we didn't pay her any mind. When that bell rang, our ears just closed right up. Half of the class was already out the door, running down the hall. I swam with the others, through a sea of children, out of the forced-open-wide double doors, down the weathered stone steps of our school.

As my feet touched the trampled grass of the schoolyard, I began to run freely. I was a speckled pony, a Bengal tiger, a blond-braided unicorn, jumping invisible fences pushing back imaginary boundaries. I swear, there is no creature so released as a child on summer vacation.

My older brother Bret was five paces ahead, a rumbling race car headed for the checkered flag which, as reality touched, would turn out to be our Mother, waiting to take us home in our wood-paneled 1959 Chevrolet station wagon. My brother Brett was bigger than me and way stronger but he couldn't run worth a lick. Even with a lengthy head start I still managed to beat him to the car.

I opened the rear passenger door and slid my bottom across the coarse woven fabric of the seat. Bret was not even a half second behind shoving me into the car as if I were an overstuffed pillow and the backseat was the pillow case.

"Hi guys," said my Mother. "Ready for summer vacation?"

"Sure are," we pealed. Bret was already pushing me off what he always claimed was his side of the backseat.

"Bret," Mother said, "I think there's enough room for two back there, don't you?"

"Yes ma'am," he said.

I stuck my tongue out at him.

"And don't you be making faces, Melly."

For a moment I sat quietly shaking my head, wondering how our Mother could drive that car looking straight ahead at the road and still know our every move behind her.

I twisted my neck backward to watch the hugeness of our brick and stone school shrink in sight and my mind's eye. By the time we had traveled the long driveway of the school and reached the crossing of the highway my eyes had to strain to keep sight of any detail. The photograph of the school which was locked in my mind from a previous thousand journeys replaced that view I could no longer see.

Samuel J. Blount Elementary School was built in 1923. The evidence of the building's birth date was deeply carved into a pale cream marble cornerstone which was lodged in the northwest corner of the structure. This was the first brick school the county had ever found sufficient tax income to pay for. It stood two stories high with row upon row of huge three foot wide and seven foot tall double hung windows. Like most of the stone-foundation civic buildings raised in the twenties, it was built with such sturdy workmanship that it should easily stand for ten thousand years. At least that's how it seemed at the time.

For when you are eleven years old and staring back at your recent escape from such an imposing monument, a building like that is nothing less than a monster.

Within seconds of our Mother pulling the car onto the main road my brother had taken up his favorite passenger-side activity. Bret stared out the car window watching the roadside as it passed briskly under his gaze. He had a keen eye and made a habit of taking mark of any discarded soda pop bottles which, should his travels on foot ever bring him this close to town, he would gather and redeem for the two cent deposit bounty. Because neither Bret or myself had a bicycle, we were forced to collect bottles within a much closer reach of home. Still, Bret took happiness in locating the treasure even if he would never have the chance to retrieve it.

For the most part we drove the eight miles from town to the farm that day in a state of truce, allowing for a couple of pokes and pinches and sinister glares exchanged. And when our Mother turned the car from the relative smoothness of the two lane blacktop highway onto the washboard orange clay road that ran the last two miles to our farm, we found ourselves busy holding onto the armrests to keep from being tossed around. The rain washed ridges into that clay road making the car shake so much your teeth could lose a filling. On top of that yellow-red clay there was a layer of fine loose sand that kicked up a choking cloud of dust which fortunately trailed behind us. Twice every year the county graded this clay smooth, and placed a sign on the shoulder calling this particular path a "Secondary All Weather Road". It didn't need a sign or a title. It was just one of a million, dusty bumpy country roads that ran across North Florida and South Georgia in 1963.

Our Mother turned left into our drive and onto our property. I gazed up, out of the car window, at the tall twisting live oaks and marveled at the way they held hands high above us creating a green canopy. Beneath this leafy parasol, Daddy had built our home--a rambling white-planked farmhouse set on red brick piers. I hadn't been born yet when they built it, but Mother said it started as a little wooden cracker box of a place with barely room for two. Mother and Daddy didn't have much money then so our Grandpa helped out with lumber, bricks and carpentry. One of the little boxes they added on was a comfortable bedroom for Grandpa to live in and stay with us. Daddy and my Grandpa kept building up and across, adding on more and more little white planked boxes till they had made a pretty nice place. After Grandpa died, which I barely remember 'cause I was only four at the time, Mother and Daddy moved into his room which had a private bathroom and I was able to take theirs. This freed me from the torture that would have been sharing a bedroom with my awful brother Bret.

As soon as our Mother brought the car to a stop, Bret-like his usually bratty self-jumped out and was fast on the move into the house to his daily after school objective, the refrigerator. Of course he had to slam the front screen door loudly along the way. Hoping to make Bret look bad, I took my own sweet time gathering myself and my school supplies before shoving the car door open with my shoulder and sliding from the seat to the ground. While my Mother was retrieving groceries from the rear of the station wagon I stepped onto our front porch. I then patiently held that same screen door open so that she could enter the house.

I can't say that I was usually all that much better behaved than Bret. Growing up on a farm turns you into a tomboy whether you're inclined to be or not. Mostly, I knew that the whole summer stretched out before me like a thousand acres of white September cotton, so there wasn't any need to hurry. I was content to meander into the kitchen, pour a glass of sweet tea into a jelly jar glass, carry it with me to my room, and hide myself away, reading until supper.

Isn't it funny how we sometimes remember every small detail of things that weren't that important at the time? For dinner that night we had baked chicken with egg noodles and lima beans. My Mother hates lima beans but they grow real easy on our land so we were always eating them. My Daddy liked them because they were hearty and he always arrived at the table hungry from working the farm. Brett didn't much care for anything green and I didn't care one way or the other. I ate the beans because...well, because my Daddy liked them.

After dinner, the stifling heat of June had yet to lessen and the sun was not near to setting down for the night. Daddy fell asleep resting his eyes for a moment sitting in his overstuffed chair. My Mother was cleaning the mess from making dinner. Bret was hiding somewhere so I went back to my room to read. Time passed by chapters instead of minutes. Eventually the sun set and the temperature became bearable enough for me to lay down on my bed. The heat had made me drowsy and the cool sheets brought me comfort that called me to flutter and shutter my eyes.

Chapter Two

Summer at our place was just one tick hotter than...well, you know the place. The red line trapped by the thermometer glass would push hard on its glass roof, threatening to burst it. Those days of June, July and August would melt through the nights one into the next. On that first full day of school vacation, I stood on our front porch with my right shoulder propped against one of the square wooden columns that held up the roof and waited for the heat to devour me. The heat of summer never came. Instead, a slight yet constant breeze blew to us from nowhere, fanning the blaze of June aside and leaving in its place a momentary sense of April. With that feint of spring came a sudden morning rain.

When it rained at our house, the drops would pound violently on our rusty tin roof. In our part of the South rain drops are so big and heavy that if you get caught outside when a storm starts it takes just seven of those drops to get you soaked to the skin. You can see why they would raise a terrible racket on a thin tin roof. Miss Crisp, our teacher, told us the roof was not made of tin but was actually corrugated and galvanized steel. She was probably right, but everyone I ever knew called

it a tin roof anyway. Miss Crisp was so darned persnickety. I
believe she said the same sort of thing about the cans and foil.

The early rain surprised me. Normally during our summers,
weeks could pass without a heavy rain, and the days of those
weeks were each as hot as the white-blue flame on a just
lit match. But that year, beginning with that odd morning
shower, summer settled on our farm as a soft gray shadowed
haze that shielded us from the worst of the sun.

I sank into a dusty white wicker rocking chair on our porch
with the noise of the rain as my music. Staring a bit blankly
into the rain I moved the rocker back and forth quickly with
my toe. The rain poured down in huge sheets that quickly
began to flood the wheel-rutted drive leading to our home.
Pools of water grew everywhere making islands of the raised
circles of earth around the trees. Sitting high and dry, I was
truly glad my Daddy had built our house several steps above
the ground. The grayness from the storm darkened to become
a drawn window shade that refused to let me see any further
than thirty or forty feet in front of me. Still, I felt as if simply
by staring into that blank curtain of rain, I could see the acres
of our farm, Blount County, and most of the world around
me.

Our farmland sat about a thousand yards into the Florida
side of the Florida-Georgia border, near Blountstown, which,
not surprisingly, is part of Blount County, Florida. At one
time, darned near half the county was owned by or named for
a Blount. Daddy always joked that one time he turned over
a big flat rock in our field, and on the bottom was written,
"Property of Samuel J. Blount."

When most people visualized Florida they didn't think of
our part, the Florida Panhandle. They imagined the palm trees
and the surf of Miami Beach, or the orange trees Anita Bryant

was always singing about. Boy, if they could have seen Blount County!

Instead of palm trees there were long needle pines, about a billion of them. Straight and skinny as number two pencils, they covered the Florida panhandle. The St. Joe Paper Company owned them all and cut them down a thousand acres at a time. In the town of Perry they had a pulp paper mill where they boiled down the timber to make newsprint. When the wind blew from the south the stench from that mill would knock you to your knees.

The uppermost reach of the famous Suwannee River passes through Blount County, but as far north as it is, it's more of a stream than a river. Somehow that lazy little river twists and grows all the way down to the Gulf of Mexico. Bret and I had never seen the Gulf back then. The only ocean of water we knew anything about came from those surprise summer rains. They didn't come too often, but when they arrived, it poured down in buckets. The heat would build for days and days until one afternoon, just in time to keep the corn from popping on the ears, those big splotchy drops would commence. And for as much rain as might pour from the sky from 3 o'clock until 7, somehow by ten o'clock the next morning the ground was back to being parched. Still, it was fertile land, and washed in turns by the rain and the sun, every crop we planted grew.

The clay road leading to our farm took a curve about a mile in from the highway and that curve cut into Georgia for an eighth of a mile. There was even a pair of signs that read, "You are now entering" and "You are now leaving, Georgia, 'The State of Adventure,'" at each end of the bend. An odd thing about that curve was that the Georgia state road crew sent a tractor all the way from Valdosta every six months or so just to grade the one little bend. That was one of what my Daddy called "life's little amusements."

Similarly, my brother Bret liked to stand with one foot on each side of the state line so he could claim to be in two states at once. I told him one day while he was doing it that he was actually in three states at one time.

"What do you mean, three states?" he asked. "My right foot's in Georgia and my left is in Florida. That makes two," and he held up two fingers on his right hand to punctuate his not so clever calculation.

"Well there's one more you're always in that you left out." I had him puzzled, and good and curious by now.

"What one is that?" he asked sincerely, unaware he had been snared.

"The state of confusion," I said with a sneer and a laugh.

"There's no state called..." he started to say, but realized I'd made a fool of him and took off after me.

I'd already headed down the road to home as soon as I said it. I could usually run faster than Bret, but that day he must have been extra bound and determined 'cause he caught me before I could reach the safety of the house. He twisted my arm with an Indian burn when he cornered me and it stung like the devil, but I tell you what, it was probably worth it.

Chapter Three

I can't say that Bret and I really got ourselves into a lot of trouble back then. I mean, we never burned down the house playing with matches or anything. We did tease each other and fight a lot. This turmoil always managed to get us on the poor side of my Mother and Daddy's wrath just about the time Sunday morning rolled around.

We didn't often attend church services, but Mother occasionally had these spells where she convinced herself that we were all going to burn in hell for lack of spiritual guidance. So, every few months or so she made Daddy shine all our shoes, dressed us up to the nines, and packed the four of us off to the red brick Baptist church in the center of town. Technically, I don't think we were even Baptists, but the only other large congregation in town were Methodists and for reasons she never bothered to share, Mother just couldn't abide with Methodist ways.

That first Sunday of summer vacation turned out to be one of those days when we were due for a dose of religion. When I awoke all ready to be lazy, I smelled shoe polish mixed with the fragrance of bacon and knew something was afoot. Within an hour of my waking and with considerable prodding along by both my Mother and Daddy I was sitting prim and proper in the back of the car on my way to what my Mother viewed as our path to redemption and I thought of as a good morning spoiled.

Daddy liked to park the car under a tree whenever he could so it wouldn't be an oven when we came back to it. But everyone else had the same idea and they had arrived before us. This gave us a walk of several hundred yards to the front doors of the church. As we walked down Main Street, I wondered what the others on their way to services thought of us, probably not too much one way or another. I mean, we weren't a bad looking bunch of coconuts.

My Daddy always said I was the prettiest girl in all of the world. I knew it wasn't true, but it was still nice to hear. I did feel pretty though, all gussied up for Sunday. I wore my second favorite dress. It was yellow with a white eyelet lace bodice, scooped neckline and an empire waist. It kind of looked like a bridesmaid's dress but not so long and formal, as the hem just came down to my knees.

I was 4' 8" tall with long shiny blonde hair that Mother was always helping me brush the tangles out of. My blonde hair gradually darkened to light brown. My eyes are blue-gray, more blue than gray. I wouldn't say I was fat, but I was definitely not tall and thin like my Mother. I guess people would say I was pudgy. Mother swore to me that she was pudgy too, and that all that pudge would end up in better places. I'm pleased to say she was right. As far as the rest of me goes, I have a light clear complexion but during the summer I pick up a few freckles on my normally pale white face and arms. I am now 5'5" and still growing.

Bret looks a lot more like our Daddy. Before Brett was old enough to shave, the only way you could see the resemblance was by the color of Dad's and Brett's hair and eyes. They both have very dark wavy brown hair and sort of green-brown eyes. Back then Bret was only a couple of inches taller than me. For some reason those summer freckles wanted no part of Bret. He could stand out in the sun all day long and never burn or tan. My Daddy, on the other hand, always looked reddish bronze, even in winter. Bret was starting to get a few muscles, and it showed, in that his shoulders were much wider than mine. He was still a typical skinny 12 year old boy, but all the tree climbing and work he did around the farm made him resemble a short young athlete (or a tall monkey depending on my mood).

As usual, the rules were different for the Fowler men than the Fowler girls. Brett and my Daddy got away with not dressing up too fancy for church. They both wore light khaki colored slacks and weren't wearing neckties and jackets like the other men wore that day. My mother had me wearing stockings, white gloves and the pearl necklace she wore to her high school prom. I carried a simple brown leather purse that was modeled after the satchels telegram boys used to carry. I had on brown penny loafers to match it.

Even though my Daddy didn't wear a dark brown suit with a kerchief stuffed into the top pocket, I still thought he was the best looking fellow in our town. Well, next to Pastor Jim that is. My Daddy was almost 6 foot tall and even when he forgot to shave, never looked scruffy. When he did get all fixed up like he did that Sunday, I think he was about as handsome as Cary Grant. My Daddy, Roger Fowler, was 32 years old that summer. He was a little wiry but not thin. Eating country meals and working a 100 acre farm without any hired help kept muscle on and fat off.

Mother was very elegant. It seemed like she was the person

I was always trying to be. When Mother wore pearls she looked like Jackie Kennedy. When I wore them I looked like Minnie Pearl. Actually, Mother was the only woman in Blount County who had opted not to wear the First Lady's look that summer.

No pillbox hat for Amanda Juliet Fowler! Mother was her own person and wore princess cut dresses that showed off her small waistline and draped across her hips. Mother had hair just a tint darker than auburn. It's a terrible comparison, but her hair was exactly the color of a chestnut thoroughbred. Her eyes were a deep blue violet, the color of the sky on a cool April morning. Her eyes were always bright and alive as if she were angry, even when she wasn't. As I mentioned, Mother was tall, taller than I am now. Mother wasn't curvy like I am, but still, she had a great figure. When Mother went shopping, men everywhere would pretend not to be looking at her.

As we walked up the red brick steps into the red brick Baptist church, that was how we appeared to be, to all the world and God's creation that Sunday that summer in June.

Chapter Four

Pastor Jim droned on and on, his dull tone driving me to distraction. I think he was talking about Vacation Bible School starting tomorrow. His words didn't seem to carry well in the oppressive summer swelter of a tightly packed church. As I used a hand-held fan donated by "Your neighbors at Brewton Funeral Home," which was printed on one side, it seemed to me that the heat had slowed the pulse of every creature in the county. The slow waft of the paper fan batted away the preacher's words, keeping them from interrupting my ponderings.

Not attending services but three or four times a year, there were plenty of things going on I couldn't make much sense of. Usually I just studied the people's clothes or the decorations on the walls and tried to hold still while pretending to listen to the preacher. In the front row there was a lady with a huge round hat which looked more like a box for a cake than something to put on your head. I would truly have enjoyed asking my brother Bret what he thought of that hat, but Mother was seated right beside him. A dozen children I knew from school appeared to be listening intently to every word the preacher spoke.

Apparently out of all the people in church that Sunday I was the only one who would rather have been somewhere else.

The building itself was rather nice inside. It had high walls with colored glass pictures for windows. When light passed through them it sent splatters of color onto almost every inch of the church's white painted walls. During the course of the service, as the sun rose higher in the sky, the red, blue and amber projections would travel from the high hewn timber ceiling, down along the walls and onto the congregation. My head turned this way and that studying the patterns of hue, while the rest of me twisted and contorted from restlessness. Mother gave my direction a stern glare of disapproval, so I shifted my gaze to the podium and made a sincere effort to pay attention.

Pastor Jim was handsome. There must be a law somewhere saying that small town southern preachers need to have broad shoulders and blue eyes. I wasn't really of an age where things of that nature held much meaning for me, but so much talk was made of the preacher's sharp looks and manner that I took the time during the humdrum of his sermon to study him. No, he wasn't bad looking at all. He had dark wavy hair that he kept slicked and a little on the long side so as to keep him in touch with the young rebels of the congregation. He was tall, with an athletic build which he worked hard at keeping trim. Most all the girls in our town had a crush on him at one time or another while growing through their teens.

I was a little startled when Mother's hand reached across my brother Bret's chest and caught my wrist, freezing the pendulum of the fan. I had inadvertently increased the speed of its motion to a point where my movement was a distraction and an embarrassment to her. She relaxed her grasp on my wrist, allowing the fan to begin again at a far more leisurely pace.

Unfortunately its effectiveness at batting away the pastor's words was now limited and a few found their way into my thoughts.

"Next Friday evening, Reverend Herbert Halliday will be holding a revival at the church picnic camp off Route 150. For those of you who are unfamiliar with the Reverend, let me give you this bit of information. Reverend Halliday is almost ninety years old and was saved by Billy Sunday himself, in the days of the old Wild West. I've heard him witness, and I can tell you first hand that his testimony is nothing less than an inspiration."

Pastor Jim rattled on and on endlessly for another five minutes about future church events and activities which I would definitely not be attending. I don't know how Mother, Daddy and Bret managed to listen politely and not be bored.

I have never been able to sit for more than ten minutes at a stretch without fidgeting and getting nervous. That Sunday in church was no different. The hard oak bench of a church pew had quickly numbed my rear to tingling. Mother kept shooting steely-eyed glances in my direction while I continued to shift myself about.

Finally her patience expired. She leaned across Bret and whispered brusquely in my ear, "You take this here coin and walk yourself to the store to buy the Sunday paper. Then walk yourself to the car and wait for us to come out and I want you to know that I'm sorely ashamed of you for misbehaving in the house of the Lord."

I solemnly slipped out of the church, but whatever penitence my heart contained left me the second I stepped into freedom and the bright glare of the noonday sun. I wasn't often allowed to walk through the center of town alone. It was Sunday though, with little traffic or commotion. Mother had given me

50 cents to take to the drugstore and buy the Tallahassee paper. All the big stores didn't open on Sunday back then, but the druggist opened from noon to two to sell newspapers and any small notion that a body didn't feel they could live without until Monday morning. The rest of the town was closed to a state of boredom.

As I walked the sidewalk jumping over the cracks, I darted between the islands of shade offered by the outstretched limbs of the trees. It seemed strange to see the town so withdrawn into itself. The First National Bank had long shades pulled down tight to the window sills. I walked past the Cozy Café, only to be saluted by a row of empty stools. A fan with streamers fastened to it had been left blowing on a cardboard cutout picture of an Arctic seal in the McCrory's window, the intent being to draw attention for a sale. Behr's Pharmacy was still a block ahead of me, their wooden screen door propped open to invite the public. I crossed Madison Street, where the sound of an electric saw buzzed through the still summer air.

John Fogarty built cabinets and furniture under two covered shelters directly behind Pierson's Department Store. Not a soul in Blountstown save old Fogie (I had a nickname for everyone) would consider working on Sunday. According to Pastor Jim, not honoring the Lord's Day was a sure path to hell, and hell, as he had minutes before reminded us, was not to be taken lightly. I allowed myself a detour down the side street to spy on Fogie's labor.

His workplace consisted of two long covered lean-tos fastened to the rear brick wall of the store. Beneath the shed-like shelter, he was engaged in planing the edge of a door, which had moments before been trimmed on a table saw. He bent over his work, stroking the wood, peeling off ruffles and whittle of curled yellow pine, his mind and soul involved in his labor.

I stole closer, secreting myself in an alcove of one of the rear store exits.

He was dressed wearing just khaki shorts, canvas shoes and a tee shirt minus the sleeves. Only a torn terrycloth headband kept his eyes clear of the sweat that poured off of him continually. Fogarty's weight would have had to be placed at somewhere between fat and blubbery. That heft, combined with the midday swelter, then added to his vigorous labor, left him huffing and puffing, gasping for breath between strokes of his plane. My Father worked that hard on our farm from time to time, but didn't carry the burden of extra pounds. As Fogarty pushed and pushed his will against that of the wood, it appeared to me that at any moment he would falter and collapse.

Then, while poised at the height of his planing stroke and the brink of exhaustion, he laid his tool aside on a workbench. Fogarty leaned his palms on the now almost smooth edge of the door and straightened a crick from his back. As he did so, the slightest, most imperceptible of all breezes began to blow through the alley. It wafted along the ground, gathering force and scattering leaves. When the wind reached Fogarty under his shed, I watched him draw from it a deep, cool breath. He stood there for a moment gathering his forces, and culling from the breeze a replenished strength. He picked up the tool and began his work again.

I slipped back out of my hiding place in Pierson's rear delivery doorway and continued on my path to purchase the Sunday paper. Somehow my lollygagging had taken so long that by the time I bought the paper and made it to the car.

Mother, Bret, and my Daddy were there inside of it waiting. The now past noonday sun had removed the car from the shade and turned it into a 1959 Chevrolet roaster toaster.

But as hot as it was in that car, I believe my Mother was at least thirty degrees hotter.

"Get in the car Princess." My Daddy always called me by a special name... even when he was upset with me. I tried to make myself invisible and enter the car, but Bret would have none of it.

"Where were you? We've been waiting almost an hour."

"It wasn't an hour, Bret. The whole sermon doesn't even take an hour." Answering Bret was a big mistake for it gave my Mother just the little push over the edge her anger had been waiting for.

"Melanie Anne Fowler we have been sitting in this God damned hot car for more than twenty minutes." Realizing she had cussed my Mother got even madder. "Now look what you made me do. Not even an hour outside of church and you lead me to taking the Lord's name in vain."

Until that day I had NEVER heard my Mother utter a single word of rough language. But sitting in that car getting hotter and hotter by the minute finally unbridled her temper. I had never seen my Mother so angry, not even when I was nine and threw a water balloon filled with India ink at Bret... and missed... inside the house. Naturally, Bret was behind that little caper but I caught all the heat. More precisely, my bottom did.

Speaking of Bret, he was sitting way over on the far side of the station wagon's back seat, biting down on his tongue to keep from laughing at all the trouble I was in. I don't know what possessed me to talk back to my Mother that day but I did.

"I didn't make you cuss, you did it all by yourself."

Mother had never struck Bret or myself ever, unless you count spankings, which don't really count. But that morning, as Daddy was driving us out of town she came awfully close. I think the only thing that saved me from getting five fingers right across the side of my face was Daddy quickly taking hold of the her hand in midair and using it to pull her over next to him. He put his right arm over her shoulder and hugged her while he drove. Every time Mother went to say something he gave her a little squeeze and said, "I know, I know."

Eventually Mother let out a big breathy sigh that sounded to me like the hiss of air expelled from a pressure cooker that had been just about ready to explode. Around the time Mother had let off her steam we arrived back at the farm. I got out of the car and went directly into my room without waiting for her to tell me I was not allowed to go elsewhere. I came out of my room for an extremely quiet dinner but immediately returned to it for an extremely boring night.

Chapter Five

Now I was sure that my teacher, Miss Crisp, had told us to enjoy our summer vacation. And I certainly had high hopes of doing just that when I woke up on Monday morning. I had figured to begin my summer with a huge bowl of Cheerios on top of which I would pour way too much sugar. Things went just fine until I was sprinkling on the fourth spoonful of sugar.

"That'll be the end of that, Melly. From now on, you use two spoons of sugar and not a bit more."

I was sitting there thinking at least I had gotten away with it that morning, when my Mother continued. "As soon as you're done with that bowl of Dixie Crystals, you're to join your brother out back of the tractor barn. You and your brother are going to plant a garden this summer."

I looked at my Mother as if to silently say, "Are you out of your mind?" Now I already told you that as far as I could see, my mother had eyes in the back of her head. But I forgot to mention she could read minds as well.

"Don't you dare be thinking that I'm out of my mind, Melanie Fowler. You and Bret are not going to loll around this farm all summer like you did last year."

Once again I answered with raised eyebrows. You see, I wasn't surprised that we were going to have chores all summer. We had chores to do all year round. No, what I could not begin to understand was why Bret and I would be planting a garden. We had an entire farm with over a hundred acres in field. The last thing we needed was a tiny hand-worked garden. I knew that if I gave my Mother one more funny look she might again forget herself and be tempted to use the palm of her hand to slap that look right off of me. So I raised my cereal bowl to my mouth and quickly slurped down the Cheerios along with the sugary milk from the bottom in a decidedly unladylike fashion. I dropped my empty bowl in the kitchen sink, and to complete my protest, on my way out back I slammed the wooden screen door, just like my brother Bret would.

It was a short one hundred feet or so out to the tractor barn. I was still under the shade of the oaks until I reached the barn. The shade only allowed a sparse grass to grow on the treed island that surrounded our house. Once you got past the shady overhang, the bright sun took over and made tall grass shoot up constantly. The tractor barn sat right at the edge of the last bit of shade from the trees.

Depending on the time of year, the roof of that barn was in or out of the sun, and was either cool or blazing. Like all of the little utility shacks scattered around our farm, the tractor barn was built of rough lumber made from trees my Daddy had cleared. I know it must seem like an impossible thing to do... that is, make planks from trees, but it isn't all that hard. Daddy used a big saw that went round and round in a loop. Anyway, you can pretty much slice up any type of tree you want with it. So, like I said, all of our barns and buildings were built out of that rough sawn wood, including the tractor barn.

That day, Bret was exactly where my Mother said he would be, planting a garden in a clear spot no bigger than a eighth of an acre. Something, or someone, must have motivated him, 'cause he was tearing up the earth with a pick as fast as he could move.

As soon as Bret saw me it didn't take a second before he was barking out an order.

"Take that rake and break up this dirt."

"You're not my boss." Back then, I must have said that to Bret a hundred times a day. He would always respond with a stupid threat of some kind or another.

This time he fooled me. He was nice. All he said was, "I know I'm not, I just want to get this done and I need your help."

Being as Bret had never once been polite to me before, I was so surprised I could barely speak. Normally, he'd have said something snotty, and I'd say something snotty right back. I mean, we were brother and sister. It's what we were supposed to do. Honestly, if he was going to be nice, I didn't know how to talk to him. I picked up the rake.

"I don't know why we have to make a separate garden by hand when we have a whole farm and a tractor."

"Daddy says we're supposed to learn how to be farmers this summer. He wants us to plant all kinds of different stuff, and sell it in town at the end of the summer."

"I already know how to be a farmer," I said. "You wake up way too early, and work way too late. Oh, and you worry about money all the time, too."

"Well, Daddy says you and me can keep all the money from everything we sell and I figure by the end of the summer I might have enough saved up for a bike."

Now I hate to think that I have a greedy heart, but the idea of keeping all the money from the stuff we could grow and sell got me working real fast. It also got me adding up our profits in my head long before we had planted our first seed. Before the week was done, I had expanded that garden in my mind to almost a full acre, and we would be growing everything from Asparagus to Zinnias. Now I knew we couldn't grow half of the crops I imagined, but the dreaming kept a smile on my face while we worked. We managed to plant almost a half acre of beans, corn, and tomatoes. In one corner of the plot I personally planted a ten by ten foot patch of Zinnias. I didn't think we could sell any, but if they turned out anything like the hundreds of different colored flowers on the packet of seeds they sure would be pretty.

Chapter Six

I thought what with working hard on the garden and staying out of trouble all week, that Mother would have forgiven and forgotten my acting up in church that last Sunday. I was as wrong as wrong can be. I suppose it was a fitting punishment for what Mother called "my shenanigans" that on Friday night I found myself seated beside my Mother under a huge canvas revival tent, awaiting the testimony of the famous evangelical preacher (though I'd never heard of him before), Herbert Halliday.

I always felt like Bret was the troublemaker in our family, but somehow whenever he did something wrong, like setting off firecrackers in a squirrel's nest or tearing a hole in the britches of his pants, it was fast forgotten. Whenever I made just the slightest slip up, all hell broke loose. That night, I started using the word hell instead of heck. After a long night listening to Reverend Halliday, I had no doubt that Hell was a very real place. Thinking along those lines, I'm fairly certain our appearance at the revival was part of some glorious plan of Mother's to save me from eternal fire and damnation. Now I am not sure if Mother felt that taking the two of us would be a little too much to handle, or that Bret was inherently good and not in dire need of salvation. In any event, Bret and my Daddy were mercifully spared from attending that night's sermons. While we waited for the show to start, I did everything but sit on my hands to keep from fidgeting about and lowering myself into even more hot water. Actually, the revival was a whole lot more interesting than a regular service. Mother and I sat on slatted oak folding chairs close to the stage in the fifth row. The first four rows sat on the sawdust floor, while all the rest had been elevated by a short wooden platform. There was a stage that was also raised slightly above the earth. The gray from age canvas tent, held aloft by three huge poles, reached high into the sky to cover us. Flaps on all sides of the tent were lifted, to allow for a cross flow of cool night air. It all so reminded me of a circus, that I half expected someone to come along with an offer to sell us a bag of peanuts.

The Reverend Herbert hadn't stepped onto the platform as yet, but over to the right side of the stage, three Negro women who called themselves "The Sounds of Joy" were singing up a storm. They were clappin' and singin', and smilin' all the while. Those colored girls kept everyone awake while the seats started to fill. Every half minute or so, someone in the audience, of which there were now almost two hundred, would shout, "Praise the Lord!" and another fellow would counter with, "Hallelujah!" With all the singin' and whoopin' it up, the whole thing was more fun than I'd have thought possible for anything related to religion. Mother told me that the Negro churches all have choirs like "The Sounds of Joy." I thought church might not be so bad if you got to whoop and holler and didn't have to set still.

Right when I was beginning to enjoy myself, the girls stopped singing. Pastor Jim walked onto the platform from behind a tent flap, and spoke into a standing microphone which whistled whenever he raised his voice.

"Thank you, ladies, for praising God with such enthusiasm." The speakers hissed on his s's. The singers nodded a smiling "You're welcome," and the pastor went right on.

They didn't usually allow black people to attend services with whites back then, but for revivals and other entertainment the rules were bent to a greater tolerance.

Pastor Jim started in. "We are truly fortunate tonight to be hearing the testimony of Reverend Halliday. I hope and pray that everyone here tonight is touched through the Reverend by God's grace. Before he speaks, let us all bow our heads in a prayer that the Word of God is heard in the hearts of us all."

Everyone lowered their eyes and prayed while Pastor Jim asked God to personally look in on our gathering. I couldn't resist opening my eyes to study all the people in attendance a moment before his prayer was over. It surprised me that quite a few others were checking on their neighbors in exactly the way that I was.

When Pastor Jim was done praying, he held up his hands to the sky as if expecting a sign from the Lord. As he did so, a short, weathered old man with a guitar in his hands and a device which held a harmonica strung around his neck stepped spryly across the stage. Allowing the instruments to hang by their cords, he smoothed back a shock of coarse gray hair, and wiped his palms on the legs of his pants. By plucking a string and turning a key on his guitar, he both brought the guitar into tune and gathered our attention. He spoke into the microphone, but his voice was so low and graveled that the speakers refused to crackle or hiss.

"Good evening ladies and gentlemen, all. I'm Happy Herb Halliday, and I'm here with you tonight by the grace of God."

A few hallelujahs popped out here and there. "I have been washed by the blood of our Lord Jesus, and because of that, I am a happy man."

He went on about the blessings God had gifted on him since being saved, such as getting married and raising children and grandchildren and such. I know it was rude of me to feel as I did, but at the time, the personal life of anyone over the age of twenty bored me beyond belief. I sighed and rolled my eyes for my own gratification. Just when I was thinking I was going to have to fidget about, old Happy Herb commenced to strum his guitar and blow his harmonica. It was supposed to be a rendition of Joy in My Heart, but the Reverend Herb seemed to lack enough air in his lungs to make the mouth organ follow a tune. After a pair of verses, he sputtered to a halt, sipped some water from a glass set on Pastor Jim's podium and began to tell his story.

"In August," he said, "I will be eighty-seven years old." A few people clapped, but Reverend Herb stopped them by raising one of his hands. "I will be eighty-seven years of age, but I was born in 1906."

We all did math in our heads while he pressed on.

"That doesn't add up right now, does it? Y'all are probably thinkin' that old man can't play the harmonica or do addition, neither."

I don't know about anyone else, but that sure was what I was thinking.

"Well strictly speaking, my mother bore me in the year 1876. But I was not 'born' until almost thirty years later."

Several Amens floated into the air.

"I was not born until I stepped out of shadows cast by men, and into the light of Christ."

Half of the audience clapped and cheered Amens and

Hallelujahs. He continued. Halliday said that in those days, he had been a bank robber out West, traveling from Arizona to Montana, robbing places along the way. There were no cars or radios and very few telephones, so robbing a bank was merely a matter of conscience and nerve. He said you needed a little bit of one and a whole lot of the other. He never said whether he'd killed anyone, but made me think that any man who had robbed as many banks and telegraph offices as he did, more than likely had. I thought of how much Bret would have enjoyed hearing him.

"On Saturday night, February 24th, 1906, I was in a saloon in Salida, Colorado, working on the bottom half of a full bottle of whiskey, when a man comes up to me and says, 'You know, Mister, you're surely going to burn in hell.' I thought it was someone I'd robbed who had recognized me, so I turned from the bar with my gun drawn to face this fellow down, and tell him he'd got the wrong man. Usually the barrel of a Colt .45 will make a man change his mind about who or what he'd seen. Well when I spun around all full of the devil's fury, the man before me just stood there and said it again. 'Sir, you will burn in the fires of hell.'

"He was standin' as still as a cactus on a windless desert night. And I was ready to shoot him right on the spot where he stood, except that in his hand he held a black leather-bound Bible, just about the size of the one I've got here."

Reverend Herb held up the Bible over his head.

"Now I'd never shot a man holdin' a Bible before, and it made me stop and think. Why, it might be bad luck or somethin'. While I was thinkin', the fellah kept right on talkin' to me and everyone else in the bar. 'If you were to die today and meet your Maker, would you know for certain that there was a place at His table waiting for you in heaven?'

"Truthfully," said Happy Herb, "I'd figured all us thieves and bandits was sort of promised to go somewheres else."

Even Mother laughed when he said that.

"Why, it made me pause for a moment and consider it all. I'd assumed I was going straight to hell the moment I died. I didn't know you could choose one for the other. The man with the Bible was marching on to something else. 'If you accept Jesus Christ as your savior, if you turn your sins over to Him, for He alone can shoulder their burden, you will be forever saved from eternal damnation.'"

Most all of us listening to Reverend Herb were pretty excited by then. We stayed at a feverish pitch while he continued to witness the moment his life had been given over to Christ.

"That man who wasn't afraid of my pistol or the bullet of any other man in the saloon that night was the legendary evangelist, Billy Sunday, and the Bible that saved both his mortal life and my immortal soul, that night over fifty years ago, is the same one I have right here in my hand."

He again held aloft the small black Bible and slowly waved it before the crowd. Quite a few more Amens spewed forth.

"Now my message for you tonight is the same one Billy Sunday had for me. The sins of man are forgiven by God. With prayer and repentance, nothing you have done in this life cannot be left behind you. Step forward, here and now, and give over your sins to the Lord. Be born again in Christ."

A tall thin man in the front row rose from his seat and, with tears in his eyes, walked onto the platform. Reverend Herb asked him, loud enough for everyone to hear, if he was ready to turn the fate of his life over to the Lord, and he meekly said, "Yes." Two more men and a lady left their seats to go forward. Reverend Herb spoke out loud as they approached.

"If anyone here has already found the Lord and wants to

renew his or her vow to God, come down and be cleansed of sin, here and now."

This was what most everyone had been waiting for. Three-quarters of the chairs emptied and lines formed to have Reverend Herb or Pastor Jim, who had joined him on the platform, lay their hands on the head of whosoever was before them and share a prayer to reaffirm their faith in the saving grace of God.

I was thoroughly surprised when my own Mother rose from her seat beside me to take a place on one of the lines. As she left, she turned and looked back to me, and her eyes said, "Well, aren't you coming?"

I wanted to go. I mean, it would have been nice to join everyone in the tears and joy of the moment, but a part of me hadn't yet decided how I felt about it all. Despite knowing my Mother would be disappointed, and suddenly feeling I was an outsider to every person present, I chose to remain in my seat. God and I were going to have to work out our relationship strictly between ourselves.

I was surprised when, on the drive home, Mother wasn't mad at me, but was really rather warm and kind. She told me that finding God was something that happened to you, not something that you happened to do.

Bret was truly sorry he hadn't gone with us when I told him how Reverend Herb had been a desperado and all. I confess that I played up the parts about the Reverend being a dangerous bandit, to make Bret all the more jealous. I have always maintained that when you have an opportunity to irk your older brother, it should be taken to the furthest extreme.

Chapter Seven

After being out late at the revival, Saturday morning found me sleepy, quiet and subdued, slowly eating breakfast. Daddy worked only half-a-day himself on Saturday and excused Bret and I from chores altogether. Usually with no school to attend, we were a couple of wild Indians racing in, out and around the house. I know this is what we most resembled because Mother accused us of it constantly. She had an odd way of telling us, too. Bret and I would enter the kitchen slamming the wooden screen door for the twelfth time in an hour. We'd pour a glass of milk from the pitcher that Mother kept covered with cheesecloth to keep the gnats and other bugs away. Running around chasing each other made us tremendously thirsty. Mother would look up from her handwork and let out a puff of annoyance. Then, she would put down whatever was in her hands. Mother always had a book or needlework or something in her hands. She'd stand up straight and tall, put her hands on her hips and say, "Y'all are actin' just like a couple of wild Indians."

Now this was in 1963, and Mother was only thirty two years old. For the life of me I couldn't see how she had ever seen any wild Indians to compare us to. There hadn't been any real Indians in our neck of the woods in about a hundred years. I think she just liked the sound of the expression. I think if Mother had been at the Little Big Horn, she would have stood straight up and said to General Custer, "Look at 'em all, actin' just like a bunch of wild Indians."

School had been closed for the summer for just eight days. This left 83 days of reckless freedom from thinking of homework and pesky boys, some of whom were kind of cute. Those 83 days left till September stretched far to my mind's horizon. Knowing I possessed an endless supply of Saturdays to draw from, I felt somewhat jaded on that particular one following the camp revival. Instead of chasing Bret from one end of the farm to the other, turning about and having him chase after me, glad for the chance to let off steam, I preferred to linger at the breakfast table and nurture a glass of milk that normally would be quickly gulped.

"Where's Bret?" I asked Mother.

"Oh, I imagine he's gone off to find a few more two cent deposits to carry into town with your father later on."

Bret made a constant habit of scouring the ditches on either side of the highway searching for pop bottles. I don't know why it is, but boys can't seem to get by without a little change janglin' in their pockets.

Rather than try to catch up with Bret, I was content to lend a hand at the kitchen sink and listen to Mother's idle chatter.

"Those two are one and the same. Your Father won't dare go into town unless he's got some folding money tucked inside the top pocket of his overalls. With the bank right across the street from the feed and hardware, he's got to haul around a big roll just to feel like he's got some money. And every time they go to town it's like they've never been before. Those two will go for hours on end looking at tractors or radios or airplane models and never buy a thing. That's why I don't go with them. I believe I'd die of embarrassment if I had to stand by and watch your Daddy almost buy this and almost buy that. You'd think the salesmen at Pierson's Department Store would know better than to waste their time after all these years of dry runs."

Not that Daddy was a miser or anything, 'cause he wasn't. Why, he was all set to buy a television from Pierson's store and surprise us until the salesman confessed that the nearest transmitting station was in Thomasville and that their signal couldn't even reach our town. You'd be surprised how many other people bought those TVs anyway just to turn 'em on and stare at fuzz. We did have a radio though and a hi-fidelity record player.

For the most part Mother was right about Daddy. And of course Bret was trying hard to follow in his footsteps. But Daddy was a little craftier than Mother gave him credit for being. For one thing, the only time Daddy ever wore bib overalls was to take those Saturday trips into town. When he worked the farm, he wore denim jeans and white cotton shirts with a collar. Daddy always considered himself as much a businessman as a farmer. Proof of this was that our little farm was completely bought and paid for. Daddy always seemed to know what crop would best show a profit. He only wore those overalls to make himself out as one of the boys.

"Well, the rest of these dishes can just dry themselves," Mother said as she placed two freshly rinsed saucers into the draining rack and walked away from the sink. "If I don't get off my feet for a spell I'll just fall down where I'm standing."

She went to a long pine chest of drawers that she always called a buffet, and drew from it her latest project, a calico quilt. Mother sat at the kitchen table and I took a place beside her.

She was hand stitching the last few diamond shaped pieces of cloth, one onto each of the cushioned little squares. She took a few stitches, her eyes intent on her work then looked up at me as if she had something she wanted to say. After three or four series of ups and downs she spoke, "Want to give it a try?"

Now I'd attempted to sew one thing or another under my Mother's guidance since I was eight years old, but never with any success. At one time I thought that if I lost any more blood from poking my thumb, I was going to need a transfusion. Regardless of how much blood was spilt, every so often Mother would try again to teach me to mend and sew. She looked at me that day with eyes that I read to say, "Why don't you try it again...for me?" I dropped my jaw and tried to find in my mind a not too flimsy excuse. My slowness to answer was taken for a yes, and she proceeded to place in my hands a needle, thread, a similar diamond shaped patch and a corner of the quilt.

"Now just take your time and keep your stitches small."

The problem with keeping the loops small was that the sewing took longer. And the longer it took, the more often I stabbed my finger. Regardless, I decided my safest choice was to go so slowly that I couldn't possibly inflict any further punishment. Mother looked up at my reasonably occupied hands, smiled and said, "You're doing just fine," and I thought, "Maybe this time I'll get the hang of it."

Placing my tongue out the side of my mouth and lightly biting down on it for balance, I slowly drew another stitch through the cloth, stretching my arm upward till the thread was finally taut.

"Have you made any plans for the summer?" she asked.

"What do you mean?" I asked, with a puzzled tilt to my head.

"Well, you're going to be footloose and fancy-free for three months. Did you plan on lolling about like last summer, or is there something particular you might want to do?"

It was odd how the expressions of Mother's Irish forebears fell from out of nowhere into her conversation. She used words like "footloose and fancy-free" or "shenanigans" all the time. She told me they were the things her Grandmother said just to get her point across.

"I hadn't really thought about it," I said. "Bret and I are working on a pretty big garden, and Miss Crisp gave everyone a long list of books to read. I guess I don't have any grand plans." I must have lingered a little long on the word grand, because Mother smiled a broad grin before she spoke.

"So you won't be going to London, England then," she said with a laugh, and the voice of Queen Elizabeth.

I joined in the game of pretend. "No, the English summers are dreadfully hot. I was thinking I might spend the season in Blountstown, Florida. It's where everyone is going this year. Have you heard of it?" I tried to make my voice sound very hoity-toity, like Bette Davis or Joan Crawford from the movies.

Mother was going to continue the game, but started to smile instead. She pulled her head next to mine and laughed the kind of laugh that was half filled with a sigh. About that time Daddy came in the kitchen door. He had on his not-quite-broken-in, think-I'll-go-to-town overalls.

"Have you seen Bret, Punkin?"

Daddy always had a different name for me whenever I saw him. Sometimes I was Sunshine, or Babydoll, or Sweetpea, but it was always something nice.

Mother answered his question. "He lit out early this morning to hunt for his treasures. I expect he's about a mile on down the blacktop road by now."

"Well, I'll pick him up on my way into town. You comin' along Sunshine?"

"No thanks, I think I'll stick around and plan my trip to London."

Daddy stared at me, and then looked at Mother, so as to ask if I was crazy. Mother closed her eyes a second and shook her head.

"Just go," she said, and stood up from our handwork to give Daddy a peck of a kiss, while pushing him towards the door. He shrugged off our silliness and went away, with Mother calling after him, "And don't you be pestering those fellahs at Pierson's store!"

I think my Daddy preferred that he and Bret spend those Saturdays in town alone. I might have been half tomboy but I suspect there are things and thoughts fathers reserve only for their sons. I didn't mind. Mother and I had plenty of secret pacts between us as well.

Mother might just as soon have saved her breath telling Daddy to not waste anyone's time, 'cause when Daddy and Bret came back from town that evening they had been to every store in town but still managed to come back empty handed.

"And Momma," Bret sometimes called Mother Momma when he was excited, "We saw a live mountain lion in a cage at Pierson's. Charlie Pierson caught it in a trap on his hunt lease."

Nowadays it's illegal to capture a wild animal like a Florida panther, but back then it was still allowed.

"Bret," said Momma (he even got me calling her Momma sometimes), "Bret, children do not call adults by their first names. What do you call Charlie Pierson?"

"Mister Pierson, but Momma he has a real lion in the cage right there in the store. Well, actually in the back near the loading dock, but it was a real one with big lion teeth just like lions in the jungle."

Now I know I'm a year and a half younger than Bret, but sometimes I thought I was twice as smart as him, or maybe he was twice as dumb.

"Bret, you are so stupid! Florida panthers are not the same as African jungle lions. First off, they're not even half as big, second they don't have manes, and third..." I didn't really have a third.

"And third?" Bret interrupted my lesson in lions to lunge directly at me with a growl and a roar of his own. "We'll see who's stupid when I catch up with you."

Once again the chase was on and I was the one in rapid retreat. I ran out the front screen door, causing the familiar sounds of the spring pulling the door shut with a slam and my Mother's sharp words, "Come back here and close this door like a young lady, young lady."

I was far enough away, out into our fields that I was able to pretend I hadn't heard her. An odd thing though, I never heard the door slam from Bret. After letting my heartbeat slowdown I started to sneak back towards the house. I rounded the corner of the tractor barn and darned if Bret hadn't snuck outside, circled that barn and come around behind me. I was positively caught and prepared myself to be forced to chew on some grass or sniff a cow patty as those were Bret's two favorite torments. Bret wasted no time in moving to grab me. He was three inches away when from behind him came my Father's deep voice.

"All right, kids!" My Daddy was a knight in shining armor! "Let's settle down for the night."

I guess my Mother had sent him out to break up the fight. He placed a hand on each of our shoulders and shepherded us back to the house.

I looked behind my Daddy's back to see Bret holding up a fist that said all by itself, "You are soooo going to get it." Once safely escorted inside the house, I sat on a small oval, looped rag rug in the living room all night long, pretending to listen to the radio, when all I truly was doing was looking at my father.

Chapter Eight

Apparently Mother had determined that our religious education would be sufficient for another dry spell, because next morning she and Daddy returned to their usual Sunday habit of sleeping in. Bret and I were left to forage for ourselves through the kitchen. As I poured cornflakes into a bowl that had an imprint of Bugs Bunny on the side, I wondered if Mother didn't start to fidget a bit herself inside when a preacher got a little long on wind and a little short on Gospel.

Bret dragged himself into the kitchen, partially awake. Once again he had buttoned his pajama top one loop off the mark. I almost laughed, but held myself back, realizing I had a mouth full of milk and cereal. A sudden burst of hysteria under those conditions usually sends whatever I'm drinking and eating rushing out of my nose. Bret took a giant old mixing bowl that he was particularly fond of down from the cupboard and proceeded to overfill it with Kellogg's cereal. From under the table my foot kicked a chair out for him to sit on. He was still half asleep and needed all the help he could get.

"Daddy doesn't like you wasting all that cereal," I said.

"I'll eat it," he said through a crunch.

"Never in a million years."

Of all the things I did that drove Bret crazy, I bet none of them bothered him as much as my snooty way of acting superior to him, which as far as I was concerned, I was.

"I said I'll eat it."

"We'll see."

I thought he might explode, so I tilted my head, batted my eyes and smiled at him with my best little girl smile to remind him it was all a game. His temper diffused and he returned to the challenge of finishing breakfast. Somehow he forced all of the cereal into himself and pronounced his victory with a resounding burp.

"Bret, you are really disgusting."

"Burp."

I knew I was defeated, so I rose from my chair and went to my room to change from my nightdress to jeans. My room was a unique blend of precious little girl and rough-and-ready tomboy. There on my bureau amidst my dolls and fluffy stuffed lion was the slingshot by which more than a few squirrels had met their demise. Inside that same dresser there were as many rocks and fossils as there were clothes.

I laid across my bed and after a minor rummaging, took from underneath it a very special prize. After turning my head to check that Bret hadn't somehow snuck in behind me, I pulled my treasure to the light, "The Secret Garden" by Frances Hodgson Burnett. I read aloud the words on the cover while studying on it the drawing of a girl my age slipping through the crack of a huge iron door. I confess that I checked this book out of the school library with no intention whatsoever of returning it on time. Of course I knew that the library rules stated firmly that all books had to be returned before the end of the school term, but I didn't care. I knew that this book would make my summer extra special. As I placed the book beneath my blouse and slipped out of the house, I thought to myself, "Perhaps I shall see London, England, after all."

Aside from our white planked cracker box house, the pole barn used to shelter the tractor and a chicken coop, the only other building of any size on our farm was a huge old barn. It was just like the red ones you see in the pictures, except it wasn't red, and it didn't have a hay loft or a weather vane on top. Come to think of it, that barn wasn't anything at all like the ones in pictures. It was just a huge peaked tin roof set on eight round poles with more of those aged gray pinewood planks for walls. When our cow, four growing pigs and all our other livestock were in the pasture as they were that day, the barn doubled as my private playhouse and castle. I walked out towards the barn with my book under my arm, walking so casually as to hopefully make myself invisible. After successfully avoiding my brother, I swung open the weathered gray planked door with just enough of a crack to slide my narrow frame through. Thank goodness the animals were outside. It would have been hard to imagine a garden of winding roses with the scent of manure drifting by.

While there was no hay loft like you see in barns in the movies, my Daddy did put a floor across the rafters that made a fine place for me to play. I climbed the rungs of the old fruit picking ladder that leaned against the second floor. I kept careful hold of "The Secret Garden" with my free hand, and hopped up the rungs of what I imagined to be a golden stair to the second floor. I then made myself comfy, propped against several stacked together sacks of feed. There was a small square door cut into the gable end of this upper floor, made so that seed and tools could be hoisted up with a rope and pulley. I opened my book, and then opened that square door to the loft barely an inch, allowing just enough light to enter and cover a page, but not for myself to be seen. There I remained in the deep trance of fiction, in a world far away, until Mother called for supper and my candle had fallen below the trees.

Chapter Nine

Monday morning, I was so sleepy I completely forgot that we were on recess, and got totally dressed for school. I wondered why Mother and Bret were biting their cheeks all through breakfast. It was to keep from laughing! I was halfway to the bus stop before I figured it out. Oh well, I never said I was perfect.

School may have been out for a season, but chores were a year-round prospect. After changing into a tee shirt and shorts, I headed on out the back door. From my place on the back porch, I had a fairly good view of our farm. It was one hundred and seventeen acres; fifty were cleared for pasture and fifty were used for planting, seventeen were deeply wooded with tall pines and short live oaks. Daddy always threatened to clear the last seventeen acres and start growing cigar tobacco on it. Whenever he mentioned or considered cutting those trees, I got grumpy and cross. I loved the wildness of the woods and it always troubled me to hear him speak of touching it.

That morning at the far end of the meadow, I saw our Daddy leaned over the engine of the tractor, shaking his head and tryin' not to cuss. In a moment he'd kick one of the front tires and say some of those words that I always had to pretend not to know. With a series of one-footed hops I skedaddled off the porch to the chicken house where I was supposed to be gathering the day's output from our dozen laying hens. Gingerly I stole the eggs from their rightful owners. I remembered a time a few years before when my Mother was first instructing me in how to gather the eggs. The hens, I learned, don't particularly care to have their eggs swiped from under them. With some of the more feisty ones, I learned to distract them with one hand while grabbing the eggs with the other. There's one other thing that's kind of important when you deal with laying hens, or any barnyard creature for that matter. You don't want to be giving all the animals names and getting real personal with any of them. Like as not, they could end up as supper some night. I tell you from personal experience, it can be darned hard swallowing a meal that used to be a pet.

If you took all my assigned chores and added them together, they only required about an hour of time. In a few weeks there would be more work to do tending our new garden but until the seeds we planted last week sprouted, our farmer's market business venture would not need any new attention.

That was the perennial blessing and curse of summer vacation, plenty of time to be bored. To deal with my boredom I fell back on that old remedy for restless kids everywhere, coloring. At eleven, I was quite an inside the lines artist. I owned a fresh box of sixty-four Crayola crayons and had several dozen three-quarter completed black outlined volumes. These were kept in a cedar wood chest at the foot of my bed. I opened what my Mother always referred to as my "Hope Chest" and removed from it both the new box of crayons and my latest acquisition, "Around the World with Barbie." I toted the tools of my trade to the living room, where

I preferred to do my coloring, sprawled on the hardwood floor of Mother's dressy parlor.

Last Christmas I had asked for one of the tall blonde dolls, which were the very latest thing. Mother turned me down flat, saying the doll was too mature for me. I still chuckle a bit when I realize now what she meant. Barbie was the first doll that wasn't flat chested. I had to make do with the Barbie coloring book, depicting Barbie fully clothed in outfits from fifty countries. After coloring Princess Barbie of Monaco and Barbie as a Dutch girl with a red tulip background, I finished a third drawing by painstakingly blending the green, red and yellow of Barbie's Scottish kilt. The sound of my Daddy clomping the clay from his feet on the porch signaled me it would soon be time for supper. Leaving the book and crayons scattered on the floor for later, I went to my room to change into clothes for supper.

Our Daddy always insisted each of us gussie up as best we could for dinnertime. He thought it was too easy, living on a farm and all, to let yourself slide to the point of looking kind of scraggly. So I took off my shorts and shirt and pulled a flower print dress over my head. Sitting at my small white vanity, I took some time to tie my hair with a blue satin ribbon. The girl in the mirror smiled and winked, her eyes the color of the ribbon. Pulling her wavy blond hair together, she deftly tied a silky bow. I powdered my face with a puff as she did hers, hoping to cover a few of our freckles. When I stood to leave, that particular Alice would disappear. As I expected, it barely took a minute before Mother called me for supper. When I entered the kitchen, Daddy who had been hiding to the left of the doorway, caught me from behind, lifting me, hugging me, and telling me I was his favorite girl.

Supper at our house was always a happy mixture of reaching,

passing and conversation. We sat 'round a heavy-legged table that was carved with swirls and flower shapes. The patterns matched the four high-backed oak chairs we sat on. The set used to belong to my Great-grandmother on my Mother's side. It's not fancy enough to be valuable but Mother claimed it was a treasure.

That night Daddy kept going on and on about his tractor.

"The only place the part's in stock is Tallahassee. I hate to waste a day traipsin' all over creation, but I can't wait a week on the mail. Even at that, I really need to eyeball the part and make sure it's the right one."

"I don't know why you go on like this, Roger," said Mother. Roger is Daddy's first name. "It's not like the state capitol is the other end of the Earth or something. The new highway can have you there in a couple of hours. The kids are out of school, so I could even go with you, if you like."

"Well, I would like to see how Hazel's gettin' on."

Hazel was Daddy's aunt, and our only living close relation. He always worried about her, but truth is, she was strong as an oak and healthy as a horse.

Mother spoke up and took charge. "We'll leave first thing in the morning. When we get there, I can look around in the stores downtown while you chase down your old tractor part. Then we'll just pick up Hazel and all have lunch."

Moses bringin' the tablets down off the mountain had nothin' on our Mother when it came to laying out a plan. She spoke with such a positive air of authority, why I couldn't even imagine anyone offering any argument. Daddy just buttered a roll and shoved it in his mouth.

Chapter Ten

Over breakfast the next morning, Mother and Daddy spelled out our chores for the day. After Mother reminded us of all our assorted duties we thought we were in the clear until she stepped off the porch and turned round.

"Bret." Mother said Bret's name like she was pulling on a piece of taffy. She stretched it out till you thought it might snap. "Bray...et, now I know you're not going to shoot off any of those fireworks you've got stashed underneath your bottom dresser drawer. Are you, Bret?"

Bret was startled by Mother's detailed knowledge of his most secret activities. "Na...no ma'am."

"And Melly, I don't want to come home and find the kitchen covered from top to bottom with butter and grease from your making cookies. You both stay close to the house and act like I'm right inside keepin' an eye on you."

We were clearly not invited on this particular outing. Bret and I didn't mind, though. This was the second full week of summer vacation, and we weren't quite ready to set still. Mother waved and Daddy smiled as the car pulled out of our drive. Bret and I sat on the front porch, waving goodbye while trying to look extremely innocent. Just in case Mother or Daddy had forgotten something and came back to get it, Bret and I waited five extra minutes after the car had been out of sight. We looked across the porch to one another and nodded so as to confirm in our minds our new-found freedom.

Then Bret and I abandoned our feigned innocence and darted around to the back of the house. We raced across the pasture toward the woodlot. Daddy's old farm tractor was a blur as I passed it. Through the brush and scrub we ran. We gave a wide berth to a fifty foot blackberry briar patch. As usual, Bret was far behind. I won every race we ever had. I could even beat Daddy, though I suspect sometimes Daddy eased up when he got close to the finish in order to let me win. Our goal was clear to the other side of our property.

Once in the woods, Bret could never keep pace with me because I was much more nimble of foot. If there was a fallen tree or a large rock on the route, I could easily leap its height or span, never losing stride. Bret had to run around the obstacles. Brain against brawn, agility versus strength, that was Bret and me.

We slammed on our brakes as we arrived at our target. It was a large round sinkhole pond planted deep in the center of our woods--green, slimy, and full of magical creatures. There were frogs and tadpoles, newts and salamanders, snapping turtles and cooter turtles. Mostly, there was mystery and the lure of a place we were expressly forbidden to explore. Of course, Mother and Daddy being gone for the day, rules such as that no longer need apply.

Bret took a long pole of a branch and drove it into the water. The pole's length was eight feet or so and most of it was underwater when it finally touched bottom. It stood, held upright by the mucky bottom as an unflagged salute to our play.

While he entertained himself by trying to knock the pole over with a well aimed rock, I scooped my hand into the cool green-tinted water and caught a tiny gray tadpole who had ventured too near to land. It squiggled and swished in my hand, filling me with an incredible, yet uncomfortable joy. The tadpole pushed and shoved, desperate to escape through my fingers. What else could I do but heave the thing at Bret?

"Yuck," I screamed, "it bit me."

Bret laughed. "Tadpoles don't bite, Melly."

Now I knew that, but needed an excuse for unloading it; otherwise Bret would think I was chicken, which actually I was. The tadpole lay on the ground at Bret's feet.

"I think it's dead," said Bret.

"Oh, no." I was filled with guilt and stooped to examine it. I poked it with my finger. The tadpole moved its tail, whipping up a frenzy. "It's not dead!" I cheered.

With the help of a magnolia tree leaf, I picked up what I hoped would someday soon be a baby frog, and lowered it gently back into the water. Instantly it swam deep and away, the water christening the tadpole with renewed life.

I still wonder what the source of that pond was. There wasn't any boil like you'd see bubbling from an underground spring. And, even if it had been fed from a small spring, there'd have to be a run for the water to pour off to. That pond never went dry. Yet, even in rain drenched months, the level of it stayed the same.

Our pond and the wood that surrounded it were the true forest primeval. Every animal was held in balance with nature by another one. A branch shorn from a tree became a floating perch for a bullfrog to sit upon and launch his sticky tongue at a passing fly who had just made a meal from the berries of that same tree. Within our seventeen acre wood were hundreds of these tiny chains, binding together the fate of every animal, vegetable and mineral. The exception, of course, was an occasional intrusion from an eleven year old girl and a twelve year old boy.

We skirted the edge of the pond, poking into this and that, until the sun stood straight in the sky. When Bret suggested lunch, I didn't argue. Playing can be awfully hard work and I had built up a powerful thirst. As we walked back through the woods, Bret put his arm around my shoulder. We were brother and sister and friends.

On reentering the pasture, there stood the familiar tractor, dead center of the field, waiting patiently for Daddy to return with its part. The tall green-brown unmown hay hobbled our legs as we crossed the field to our porch.

"What should we have for lunch?" Bret asked.

"Peanut butter and jam for me," I told him.

Yesterday, Mother had opened a jar of her home-canned strawberry jam. That, piled in between two pieces of bread with some Skippy, was my kind of meal. We sat on the front porch, chewing our sandwiches, washing down every other bite with a huge gulp of milk.

I looked at Bret, thinking about how much he and Daddy were alike. They both had very wavy, dark brown hair. Bret wore his in a flattop crew cut so no one could tell it was secretly curly, but he hadn't been to the barber in a month, so its true nature showed. He had Aunt Hazel's light gray eyes, and though you couldn't see it in him then, he would be tall like her and Daddy.

We were still sitting on our gray-painted planked porch, cooling our heels, when the twilight of dusk surrounded us. I entertained myself with a ball and jacks. The trick with jacks in Florida during the summer is to drop the ball, grab some of the little spiked stars, and take a swing at a few mosquitoes, all in one quick move. For similar entertainment, Bret had a little pink Spaulding ball that he could amuse himself with for hours on end by tossing it against the steps of the house and catching it on the bounce. He liked to pretend he was Mickey Mantle.

Chapter Eleven

We sat and we waited for another hour, watching the dirt drive for the lights of Daddy's car. Mother had said they would be back in time for supper, which, with the sun now on its way to Alabama, would make them about ninety minutes late. I hoped their delay was from too much time spent shopping. Mother always brought me home a blouse or skirt or some ladylike thing from these trips. Daddy in turn usually bought Bret some baseball cards for his collection.

I was just ready to turn on the porch light, in order to begin another game of jacks, when the bright amber beams of headlights came bouncing up and down in the distance. It was now pitch black out. The moon was in its crescent and the tree limbs overhead had blocked its slight remaining glow.

If my recall of what happened next is twisted about, understand that the following days were a contorted zigzag jumble. All of my feelings were wrestled till they tore. Nothing was right. Nothing was the same.

It was dark, so dark that when the car pulled in, I didn't see the star painted on its door. It wasn't until the tall man left the car by himself that I realized it: this wasn't Mother and Daddy's car.

"Are you the Fowler children?"

"Yes, what can we do for you?" said Bret, as I scooted over to his side.

The man shone his flashlight on the door of his car, revealing the sheriffs' emblem on it.

"I'm Deputy Sheriff Collins. I was sent out to pick you all up." He spoke to us softly, almost like he was ashamed to talk.

"We're supposed to wait for our parents," Bret offered. "They'll be here any minute if you want to wait."

The deputy shook his head and bit on his breath.

"I'm sorry, but I need to bring you into town to talk to some people."

"Where's our Mother and Daddy?" I asked him. "Are they in town?"

He didn't answer.

"Where are our Mother and Daddy?" I demanded an answer.

"Look here, everything's going to be fine, but for right now you need to ride into town with me." He didn't look at us when he talked, he just kept turning his head this way and that, never letting his eyes rest. It was all so terribly strange.

"Come on and ride up front with me." He made a weak smile and opened the front passenger door.

It was now 9:00 o'clock and I was tired just from waiting. I got in the car and Bret slid in beside me, looking terribly scared. All the bits and pieces are still such a tearful blur to my mind. I recall the deputy told us his first name was Tom and tried to make some idle talk. Mostly, I remember jostling around on the seat as we drove the two miles of washboard clay road to the highway. I remember the brightness of the lights from the oncoming cars piercing my glassed over eyes as we rode the last six miles to town. I remember holding Bret's hand so tightly that all of the life inside me poured itself out into the grasp of his palm.

Deputy Tom parked the police car directly in front of the big brick Baptist church in town. Looking through the car door window, I noticed that the arched wooden doors of the church were propped open, allowing the cool night air to enter and releasing to the night the combined brightness of the building's electric lights. The deputy came around to open our door. Taking us each by the hand he led us into the church.

Despite there being at least a dozen people standing in the back of the church talking, I didn't recognize a single soul save one. The one face I did know was Jim Wilson, the good looking church pastor.

He quickly came over to us and introduced a very pretty blonde haired lady who was with him, as his wife. We all sat down on a church pew. He sidled up close and held my right hand in both of his. His wife sat next to Bret with her arm around his shoulder. The pastor and his wife spoke in hushed tones. They told us that the Lord is so great and so grand that ordinary people just can't understand why he does the things he does. They told us that Mother and Daddy had died.

His wife bit down hard on the knuckle of her left hand. I stared at her and the preacher for the longest time. I looked at them both, certain they had lost their minds. And then I said so.

"I know you're a church Pastor and your not supposed to lie, but you must be mixed up. Our Mother and Daddy just went off to Tallahassee for a tractor part. They'll be back home at our farm any minute now."

Perhaps because Bret was older than me, or maybe he thought I was too young to understand, but Pastor Jim turned to Bret and spoke as if I were no longer there.

"Bret, there was a terrible accident on the new highway in the rain. Ten cars crashed. One of them was your parents' station wagon."

Bret was having not one bit of it and I didn't blame him.

"First off," Bret said with anger, "it wasn't raining out and hasn't rained a drop all day."

"It was a sudden thunderstorm twenty miles away," spoke Pastor Jim's wife, who was now speaking directly to me, and stroking my hand as if it were the broken wing of a tiny hurt bird. "All the people weren't used to driving so fast on the new interstate highway."

I couldn't understand why they were saying these things that couldn't possibly be true. Then, I looked up over the height of the church pew in front of me. A dozen other people had come inside the church. There were three women and a man in the front and a larger group off to my right, and they were all crying. The man with the three women was old Fogie and even he was crying. I could see no reason that he would be there unless something of some kind was truthfully wrong.

"No, no, no," I cried inside. "I don't believe you!" I cried outside. I beat my hands on the preacher's chest as hard as I could. I railed and wailed in broken defiance. I sobbed and sobbed, over and over, hearing murmured comforts from Pastor Jim and his wife mixed with the angry voice of my brother.

"You're lying!" he screamed in furious anger. "How could they be dead? They just went to Tallahassee for a tractor part. They'll be ba....back any minute. You'll see."

I raised my eyes hopefully.

Bret and I wept through the night, arguing constantly that what they said was true simply couldn't be. We told them again and again that Mother and my Daddy were in Tallahassee, buying a part for the tractor.

The preacher Pastor Jim, his wife, and the deputy stayed with us, tirelessly explaining about the accident while sharing as best they could all our tremendous sorrow. Sometime during the early morning darkness the other people who had come to the church for their share of the tragedy nodded to Pastor Jim so as not to disturb us and drifted out through the doorway.

Pastor Jim's wife dimmed the lights over the pews and closed the doors to the church. She suggested to Pastor Jim that we all go to their home and as soon as I heard her say that I wrapped my arms around Bret who then wrapped his arms around the end of the pew. We had no intention of going anywhere until Mother and Daddy came for us.

Despite my constant yawning I managed to stay awake through the night. Eventually sunlight sent a message of morning through the church's stained glass windows. A quiet submerged part of me forced itself to admit that dawn had come and Mother and Daddy still had not arrived. That thought was the damnation of my hope.

Chapter Twelve

Our Great Aunt Hazel arrived on the Trailways bus the following afternoon. Somehow she dragged our hearts and bodies through the funeral services. I was little more than a black clothed ragdoll propped upright by Aunt Hazel and several sympathetic mourners. As I try to focus my mind on the days following the accident, a picture comes to me of Aunt Hazel, holding my white gloved hand in her white gloved hand, standing tall and erect at my side. I couldn't stand to look at Mother and Daddy's graves so I looked away from the service, upward, deep into her eyes. They were so gray and bland, so unwilling to betray her thoughts and feelings. I think now that she must have stood at gravesites many times before. I close my eyes and see her clearly, staring forward, bravely exhibiting a practiced and dearly bought strength of spirit.

My Father's Aunt and our Great Aunt Hazel was a person unlike any other. To begin with her appearance was nothing less than daunting. Hazel Fowler was almost 6 foot tall and always wore a sturdy two inch high heeled shoe. Hazel was thin to the point of resembling one of those long-legged birds that live in the marshes along the coast. She was a great blue-gray heron.

At the age of 63 she still wore her hair in exactly the same bobbed style as she did in the 1920s. Being born in the year 1900, her 20s were also the "Roaring Twenties." Great Aunt Hazel was a thoroughly modern woman of her day. She attended the Florida State College for women where she studied prelaw and marched for the right of women to vote. When she married, being a true suffragette, she kept her maiden name which was unheard of and almost illegal at the time. Some days she was warm and friendly, others she was cantankerous as a snapping turtle, a 63 year old snapping turtle. She had an opinion about everything.

My only earlier encounter with Hazel of any length of time had been during a summer vacation when I was nine years old. My parents had shipped me off by bus to spend a week away from farm life. That was an odd week during which I got to see the side of my great aunt that was formed by the blend of her progressive nature and her conservative upbringing.

Indeed, she was and is still a peculiar bird, my great aunt. Twice each week her Negro maid would arrive to do the cleaning. Given Aunt Hazel's penchant for cleanliness there really wasn't anything to wash or pick up or polish. Still, she eagerly awaited Lila's arrival every Monday and Thursday. Lila was, although I'm loath to admit it, a stereotype of the southern black maid. She was more than a little on the heavy side and wore over her hair a kerchief in the exact manner of the famous lady on the pancake box. Lila had been coming to my aunt's home to clean up nothing for over twenty years.

Aunt Hazel would anxiously pull down from her cupboard a separately stored dainty white china cup and saucer moments before Lila's arrival. She explained to me that it wasn't proper for white people and black people to mix such things as the cups they drink from.

Yet, twice a week for twenty years, she would sit and chat for four hours at a stretch with Lila, graciously filling that delicate bone china with cup after cup of coffee, making the two of them lunch and sharing between themselves any confidence.

That was and is dear crazy Aunt Hazel, a series of contradictions, the exception to every rule.

When the funeral ended we were driven to the farm in a long black car furnished by Brewster's Funeral Home. After riding in that car crying into my handkerchief all the way back to our farm, I swore I would never touch one of their damned fans in that Baptist church again. I was blazingly angry at God and everyone else, so a trip back to the brick Baptist church was not very likely. Bret sat facing me on a small seat that looked backward as we rode. His eyes stared intently out to the gutter of the road, picking out empty soda pop bottles that he would never come back to collect. Aunt Hazel took the time while we travelled to close her eyes and rest. At least that's all I thought she was doing until I saw several long trails of tears running from her eyes to the bottom of her chin.

We went home to the farm--Aunt Hazel, Bret, and myself-- where I discovered in myself a new-found listlessness of spirit. Endlessly, I sat on the front porch steps with my legs stretched downward. Bret sat across their landing, above and behind me, his face drawn long and tight. We were perfecting the art of sadness. All of the things we liked to do such as play ball and chase around the farm were nothing but sad reminders of our loss. We sure weren't ever going to play jacks or pretend to be Mickey Mantle ever again. Aunt Hazel would play the radio, and music would drift on the still summer air, out to the porch where we continued to sit for days and nights. Just one summer before, my Daddy had danced "The Twist" with me right on that same front porch.

If a song came on that my Daddy used to happily sing, like Ramblin' Rose or Honeycomb, I would get up off my bottom, march into the kitchen and turn that radio off in such a way that warned it, that if it played one more of my Daddy's favorite songs it would end up at the bottom of the pond.

While we sat around rightfully feeling sorry for ourselves, Aunt Hazel cooked for us and tended to our chores. Our cow got milked and enough of the chicken eggs were gathered for breakfasts and baking. With less people to feed, around half of the eggs became peeps that were soon scampering everywhere. We didn't have a cat, but I was angry enough to wish we did.

The business affairs of our parents' death were all tended to by Hazel, who never mentioned to us a word of it all. To this day, I don't know what happened to the wreck of our station wagon, or who paid most of our bills for those summer months. I suppose it was Hazel, but she's not of a mind to talk about it. She's never been one to dwell in the past.

When Hazel was twenty eight she married William Farrell, the son of a farming family that lived twenty miles north of Tallahassee. Just two years into her marriage, her husband came down with rheumatic fever and left her a young widow with nothing but a mortgaged fifty acre cigar tobacco farm. Three days after her husband's funeral my Great Aunt Hazel put her clothes into a satchel and walked all the way into town. Inside of a month she had traded that farm for the house she lives in still. Hazel has never been the kind that stands frozen by regret or sadness.

Blountstown being such a small place, everyone knew our trouble. For over a week, we would wake to find baked goods and groceries in bags by the door. It was truly kind of everyone, but it made Bret and me see ourselves through the eyes of the donors. We were the poor orphaned Fowler children.

A still half-green leaf from one of those shade oaks above us broke loose of its twig and fluttered to earth. In the time it took to fall, it seems another week had passed and found us still sitting in our same positions on the porch and steps. We stared fish mouthed at the sight of Aunt Hazel standing in the doorway with her satchel in hand.

"Children," she announced, "I'm going home."

We couldn't believe our ears.

"I told the mailman to have a taxi sent for me at nine this morning," she continued. Our mailbox was out on the blacktop highway and Hazel must have hiked the two miles out to it in order to ask the mailman to send the cab.

We didn't have a home telephone. The Blountstown phone company had only a party line in service for our part of the county. Six families shared that one connection, answering to a specific series of rings. We tried being the seventh for a while, but with so many people sharing the line that ringer box just never kept quiet. Mother said it broke on its own, but I think Daddy got mad at it one day and tore it clean off the wall. I was only six when it happened so I can't really say. Anyway, Daddy had the company disconnect it, telling them that when the phone company could see its way clear to run a few more lines out to our road, then he would give it another try. If we wanted badly enough to talk to someone, we loaded up the car and drove to town. The rest of our business with the world was carried on by mail.

What a sight Hazel was, standing on the porch in an ankle length skirt and starched white high collared blouse. With her carpetbag satchel in one hand and closed umbrella tucked under the other, one would have thought her an elderly Mary Poppins.

"Why didn't you tell us?" I asked.

"There was no need to get everyone riled up last night."

"Who'll take care of us?" I asked.

"You will, I suppose," she answered. "You'll take care of yourselves, and you'll take care of each other."

I started to cry, and I was tired of crying.

"I have to get home to Cleo and Caesar," she said, a bit more compassionately then her last round of words. Cleo and Caesar were her cats. "The neighbors can't take care of them forever, no more than I can watch over you two."

I couldn't believe it. She was leaving us for a couple of mangy, overfed cats.

"You both could come home with me, if you've a mind to." For a moment the prospect of a wing to be sheltered under held an appeal, but leaving the farm would have meant accepting that Mother and Daddy would never come back to us. That was something I wasn't near prepared to do. My urge was to hide, not to run.

"I'll write to you once a week to check up, but it's time you both had something to do. Taking care of this farm and yourselves is probably just the ticket."

The taxi pulled up and Aunt Hazel quickly settled herself in the backseat. She rolled down the window and motioned me over. She shaded her eyes with her white gloved hand, though the sun was still trapped behind the roof of the house.

"Melanie," her voice was cracked and dry, "the Lord sometimes decides a child must grow up before he...or she has rightly come of age. It's as if the Lord freezes the ice on a fast river and dares you to walk across. You might not be able understand why He froze the water, but you know a bridge when you see one. As much as my heart wants me to stay here and hold time still for you, I can't. My prayers and their answers tell me I need to do something else."

Aunt Hazel took that moment to blow her nose for the longest time before she spoke again. "All right driver, you better go now."

The tires of the taxi churned in the drive, filling the air with dust. I watched it trail the yellow cab a mile into the distance. I was eleven years old. It would be nine more years till I had any idea what my aunt had meant. I'm still not certain if she left us for our own good or merely out of eccentricity. When I did come to terms with her words, I would easily forgive her for leaving us. But that morning, I stomped around the house, fuming mad. Bret, who hadn't seemed all that bothered about Aunt Hazel leaving, was seated in the dining room, leaning back, balanced on only the two rear legs of a chair.

Chapter Thirteen

"Mother doesn't like you sitting like that..." Oooh, I caught myself too late. I couldn't believe I said that. I drew a chair, sat, and put my forehead straight down on the table. I was absolutely dizzy. My brain reeled and my breath turned into a series of huffs and puffs. I rolled my eyes upward to see Bret clenching the edge of the table to keep his balance, while quietly, painfully, crying. Every ten seconds or so, he would wipe his eyes on his shirt sleeve. I saw then that Bret's pain and grief were far greater than my own.

Bret slammed the front chair legs down hard, crashing them onto the floor. He bolted away. The back porch screen door swung wildly open and shut as the only evidence of his passing by. I leapt up to follow. My eyes caught him running madly across the pasture. I pushed the door out of my way and as fast as I could ran after him.

When I reached him, he was at the tractor, which was still sitting in the center of our field, exactly where Daddy had left it. Furiously, he kept slamming and heaving his weight against it.

"Help me Melly, we've got to get this stupid tractor into the barn. The rain will just rust it away."

I didn't see why he was so bent on moving it, especially at this of all times, but it seemed to be the only thing in the world that mattered to him, so I joined in his futility.

The hay grass had grown in the meadow three feet high. I stomped it down in the area of the tractor, creating a work space. Bret had his back pressed to one of the rear wheels in a useless effort to turn it forward and move the green and yellow beast a fraction of an inch. I copied his movement on the other wheel. The tractor seemed to cruelly laugh at us. The grass reached up with invisible claws, holding fast to the tires, goading us to a mutual anger. Bret was too angry to stop pushing, but I found a small place in my mind that was calm and willing to accept a thought.

"I know what we need," I said to myself. I thought of how, in our science class, we had used ropes and boards to lift things that were so heavy I could scarcely believe moving them was possible. Mary Dunleavy had pushed on the long end of a board propped over a barrel and lifted the three heaviest boys in class clear off the ground. I ran to the barn and back to the tractor, dragging behind me a long spare rail for the fence.

"Help me put this under the axle," I ordered.

Bret looked as if all his suspicions of my insanity had finally borne fruit.

"Help me slide it under the tractor." I gritted my teeth as I spoke. "In school we learned...an old Greek fellow named Archimedes once tried to move the whole Earth with a lever." I don't think I had that part of the story straight. "We ought to be able to roll this damn tractor." Oops...that was a slip on my part. I think that tractor had a way of inspiring people to cuss.

Bret, finally tired of mindlessly throwing his small human

frame against the bulk of the huge steel machine, came over and helped me. We managed to slide a third of the length of the rail under the axle. With our bodies stooped and an end of the rail on our shoulders, we pushed upward.

"Eeah!" screamed my brother. We doubled our efforts, lifting and pushing harder.

"Mooove," we exhaled, as we straightened our backs to the task. We struggled and strained upward.

The tractor moved. The wheel we were pushing rolled forward less than four inches, leaving a tire tread footprint as proof of our progress. In it an earthworm squirmed, having lost its hiding place. We didn't cheer our success. Instead, Bret returned to his state of angered determination, chucking the rail under the opposite side, and began to repeat the struggle. We strained against the yoke of the pole. The tractor moved again. Push by push, foot by foot, we rolled the tractor towards the barn. After we had moved the tractor ten feet or so, Bret laid flat boards under the front wheels to make it roll a little easier.

I forced Bret to take a break for lunch. Neither of us felt like talking. After sandwiches and a few glasses of cool well water, we took up our job where we'd left it. Eight hours after starting, we closed the doors to the barn, with the tractor parked inside.

It was pretty late, the time of day I always called dark-thirty. The house was empty of light. No one had been home to turn the switches on. We stumbled into our rooms, our bodies beyond exhaustion, and then fell onto our beds, asleep before we landed.

Chapter Fourteen

Sunlight splashed against my eyelids, waking me. I yawned, stretched, and blinked the sleep out of my eyes. Ever so gingerly, I rose, completely sore from yesterday's labor. Leaning my elbows on the window sill, I stared outward, a Dorothy surveying her Kansas. The wind blew across our meadow, pushing the tall grass to one side as though some giant's comb had neatly placed a part in it.

"Time to make breakfast," I spoke aloud to myself. I shuffled my feet along the wooden floors of our house, aiming myself in the general direction of the kitchen. There lived Old Smokey; yeah, I guess I put a name to just about everything around that farm. Old Smokey was our black iron and white porcelain-handled wood stove. I opened the lower cast iron latch and tossed in a few pieces of kindling. Striking a match on the stove top, I reached inside and started a flame. The kindling caught quickly and I snatched my hand out to safety. Old Smokey was a good stove, but not to be trusted.

Minutes later, a black cast iron skillet crackled with cooking sounds. Country ham and eggs smothered the house with their fragrance.

"Smells good." Bret had dragged himself from slumber, lured by my secret weapon, breakfast. I handed my brother a plate of eggs and ham.

"Did you make biscuits?" he asked.

"You're dreamin'," I told him. "I only bothered to make eggs for you because I had extra." The war between brother and sister was herewith resumed.

"It's just as well. Too much of your cooking would likely poison a man."

"You don't seem to be suffering any," I said, watching his fork tear into it.

"I'm trying not to hurt your feelings."

He actually had the nerve to say that with his mouth stuffed with the eggs I had cooked for him. I reminded myself to burn his eggs tomorrow morning. I do so love a good bickering.

In the week that followed, we began again to write our lives on the blank pages of summer, filling them with an occupied lament for Mother and Daddy. We put ourselves to the many tasks at hand, namely chores. The ordeal and triumph of moving the tractor into its barn had done nothing to feed the chickens, gather the eggs, or milk our cow (who was named Rosie, because milking cows don't have to worry about being slaughtered for supper). Plus, there were four pigs, three geese, and fifteen turkeys in a pen, getting fat for sale in autumn.

Still, there never seemed to be enough busywork to keep me from remembering. I roamed the hallways and rooms of the house, poking into drawers and cupboards, looking for bits and pieces of Mother and Daddy. Sometimes I would cry after merely passing their room. Other times, I would sit on the edge of their bed, the quilt Mother and I had sewn resting beneath me. My mind would wander fairly painlessly over my reminiscence. I avoided thoughts of holidays or birthdays, but the pictures of day to day living with Mother and Daddy seemed to comfort more than bother my heart. I sat on the corner of their bed for hours, thinking of everything and everyone.

I wondered about Bret. These days he channeled all of his spirit into work on the farm, everyday sounding more to me like Daddy. It was even getting hard to start a good fight with him.

Our isolation was interrupted only by a weekly letter from Aunt Hazel. I didn't answer her writings, for as far as I was concerned she was a deserter, and should be treated only as such.

Her letters rambled from one idea to the next, like a "Mad Hatter" in ink. "When my William died, the farm was way too much for me. I could no more run that place than sprout wings and fly. Oh, there's Cleo scratchin' at the door. Be right back. Okay, that's better. Darn cat. As I was saying, I got myself dolled up as best I could, and headed into town, and I never looked back. Did I tell you your cousin Lenue was coming to stay? He's going to the college this fall and going to be my boarder....."

Her letters went on like that for three pages or so. She would close the letter when a cat or mailman or sparrow or any little thing called away her attention. She'd sign, "Uh oh, gotta go, love, Aunt Hazel," till next week's letter, which would pick up wherever the last had quit. Oh well, the letters gave Bret and I some common ground to share besides our chores.

"She says we need to take some money from the cookie tin and pay the electric. She says if we don't know how much it is, to mail them fifteen dollars and that should cover it. Bret, are you listening to me?"

Here was Bret not six feet away from me and hadn't heard a single word I said. I reeled my foot back and presented him with a swift kick in the shin. His slight reaction was to reach down and rub his calf with his hand. He looked in my direction quizzically as if to say, "You kicked me, didn't you?"

Instead of mentioning my kicking his leg, he looked at me and said, "What...Melly did you say something?"

"Yes I did, I asked you about the electric bill. Do you know how much it comes to?"

"I don't care, I don't use the lights anyway."

If Bret got any more sullen, I was going to scream. He ate. He worked. He slept. I kept wondering, where was my brother? This was not the guy who set new standards of mischief, which to this day are unmatched. Where was the Bret who had hidden under feed sacks in the loft for three hours, just for the chance to scare the bejeezuz out of me so bad that I fell out of the loft 8 feet to the ground? Where was my evil brother who had actually dug a 4 foot deep tiger trap covered with pine straw and filled with mud, with me as the intended tiger? What a feeble trace of fire burned in his eyes. Is that the rite of passage to adulthood, I wonder, permitting your disappointments to dampen the flame of life? I thought that day, though not in these terms, if that is the price of growing up, then I would be Peter Pan.

As to Bret, I set about to annoy and provoke him, until I received a response that would be less than businesslike.

"Bret," I called slyly, "could you come in here?" I was in his room. Normally, this in itself would drive him to the brink of fury. But these days he didn't hardly notice. He passively entered the room. "I knocked this model plane off the dresser, cleaning, and a piece fell off."

Bret had collected pop bottles off the highway for a month to buy this plane. I figured he'd at least scream at me.

"Try to be more careful next time," he said gruffly, and put the busted plane away in a drawer. This was going to be tough.

Bret went outside to fix the turkey pen, or build a dam for the T.V.A., or something. I sat at the kitchen table, drumming my fingers, carefully plotting my next move.

Chapter Fifteen

"Bret," I called him, "I made lunch." There are only two things in the known universe my brother will not eat. One is beef liver. The other is rhubarb. Rhubarb is a tart half wild plant that grows in sunny patches here and there on our farm. It is so sour that most people only use it in pies, mixed with strawberries, made with plenty of sugar. And calf's liver is... Well, I guess everyone knows what that is. Anyway Bret would never eat either of them. No matter how they were prepared he hated them with a passion.

I made them both, together. This was perhaps the only liver rhubarb casserole ever baked. It was as horrible a meal ever created.

"This should get a rise out of him," I thought.

Bret sat at the kitchen table, his face hollow, his eyes especially blank. I placed my creation on the table and pulled off its tin foil cover.

"Voila!" I sneered. "That's French for surprise, you moron."

He studied the contents of the chaffing dish for only a second until its pungent aroma reached him. He was not happy.

"What the hell is this?"

Up to that day I had never heard Bret cuss, and to this day I haven't since. I had hoped my culinary disaster would get him back to being his old stinker of a big brother self. I know now, though, when someone isn't in the mood for a joke, a not-too-funny one will drive them clear to the edge of madness.

Bret swept the dish off the kitchen table with the back of one arm and lunged at me from his chair. I ran for dear life. As quickly as I was out the door, Bret was up and after me. I ran across the meadow, two acres of which Bret had actually cut by hand with an old scythe he found in the barn. I had a hundred foot lead on Bret, but I could tell he was catching up. His hollering kept getting closer.

"Melanie Fowler, I'm going to whip your bottom."

I ran a little faster.

"I'm going to whip your bottom raw." I really think he finally meant it!

I wanted him riled up, but not raving mad. Darting left, I cut for the woods. Jumping over fallen logs and bushes, I was able to keep a little distance ahead. Bret was still back there yelling. I passed around the wild blueberry and blackberry briar patch and through a small stand of pines. Finally I reached my target, the green slimy pond.

We hadn't been to the pond since the day Mother and Daddy left for Tallahassee. This wasn't on my mind as I ran to the far side, putting the water between Bret and myself. Bret jumped left, and I jumped left. He moved right. I moved right. He soon tired of running around the pond in circles and chose a vocal attack.

"When I catch you, I'm going to punish you good."

"You're not my boss," I taunted him. "You're nobody's boss."

"I'm the man of the house now, and you have to mind what I say."

I laughed, "Ha! I don't have to mind you. I don't even have to look at you." With that, I turned away, lifting my nose in the air real snooty-like.

Bret thought I could be caught off guard, and made a quick dart for my side of the pond. I figured he'd try that and just when he leapt to grab me, I jumped out of the way.

Unfortunately, the spot where I had stood was a little too close to the edge. When Bret landed, the bank of the little pond caved in, tumbling Bret into the water. That was the good part. The bad part was that the stinker had somehow managed to catch hold of my shoe with one hand while falling into the pond.

Now our pond is a lovely place to visit, and explore the wonders of nature, but like the saying goes, you wouldn't want to live there. Thank God we both had been topnotch swimmers for years and had no problem paddling over to a low hanging branch to quickly pull ourselves up and out. We flopped like two freshly caught catfish onto some mossy ground, safely out of the water.

Bret was covered with thick green algae. "Arrggh, a swamp monster." I pointed my hand at my now deep green brother.

Bret laughed and howled, rolling about on the moss, completely amused. He tried to talk, but he couldn't seem to straighten up long enough.

"You don't look that funny," I told him. Though, truth is, he did.

"I'm not laughing at me, Melly." I was a bit puzzled. "I'm laughin' at you." He attempted to point a hand at me, but a convulsion of giggles overtook him.

I was as green as Bret. Worse yet, a clump of hydrilla plants had caught in my hair, giving me a set of antlers and the look of a midget green swamp moose. I know this is how I looked, because my dear brother pulled himself together long enough from a spurt of hysterical laughter to tell me so.

"Arrrgggh, the swamp moose!" he cried out, and collapsed on his back for another round of hysterics.

Even though I was covered in slime, I had to admit it was all pretty darned wild and funny. I wonder if laughter doesn't somehow relight that flame?

We laughed. We laughed harder than anyone had ever laughed before. I'd sit up and see Bret. He'd see me, and off we would go again, rolling on that moss, snorting and sniggering as if some unseen hands had grabbed us by our middles and tickled us raw. Bret laughed so hard he cried. I laughed so hard I peed my pants.

We had not laughed out loud in so long. Not since that last trip to the pond. True, less than a month had passed since Mother and Daddy had died. But when you stop laughing, time does not so funny things.

Eventually, we wiped the green off of each other and started walking home. Water squishing in our sneakers kept perfect pace with our footsteps as we passed across the meadow.

That evening after bathing and changing into clean duds, we sat at the kitchen table for a simple family supper of canned Campbell's soup and homemade bread from our deep chest freezer. The somber spell that had taken a hold of Bret seemed to have been broken. We chatted away for hours, passing across the table remnants of our parents' conversations we had heard all the years before.

"Those turkeys are putting on weight real good," Bret would say.

"Well, they should, as much it costs to fatten them up," I respond.

"The hens haven't been layin' too well,"....Bret.

"I don't know as you could expect them too, what with it bein' summer and all,".....me.

"That's true enough, I suppose,"....Bret.

"Sure, just a little hen heatstroke,"....me.

We both chuckled lightly and continued our patter, finding a genuine solace in the familiar ring of our words. On we chattered until sleep called, and casual conversation lent itself better to a series of warm goodnights. I fell to a sound sleep easily.

Chapter Sixteen

"Rise and shine, Melly."

A voice poked a hole in my sleep. I opened my eyes, and there was Bret, dressed like the hayseed farmer he was. His overalls were slung on one shoulder, hillbilly style. He was barefoot, and had rummaged up a big old floppy straw hat.

"Halloween so soon?" I asked.

He laughed and turned on his heel. His voice traveled from the kitchen. "Breakfast is made."

Disregarding the fact that brother-dear had never successfully boiled water, I rose and treaded towards the pantry. Along the way, I passed under a brown paper banner that read, 'Bret's Country Kitchen.' The kitchen was quite a remarkable sight. The table was covered with a blue checkered cloth, and, wonder of wonders, the places were set. Bret pulled out my chair and placed in my hand a hastily written menu. I was in awe of him. When I opened the menu, I realized that Bret was more aware of his limitations than I had given him credit for. Every item was the same. There was Cereal, and Cereal with Milk. There was Milk and Milk with Cereal.

"I'll have the Cereal with Milk," I said, pointing to the second line.

Bret, playing the part of a waiter, whisked the menu out of my hand and commented, "A wise selection, madam."

"Aw, Bret, sit down and pass the Cheerios."

We spent the next three days fading in and out of characters, pretending to be all manner of people and creatures. I spent one entire day pretending to be a lady in waiting at the court of King Arthur. To his credit, Bret was better than a good sport and acted the part of a knight. Of course, his cooperation bound me to do likewise when he wanted to play soldier.

"Corporal Melly reporting for duty, sir." I gave him a sharp salute.

"At ease, Corporal, are you ready for inspection?"

"Yes sir."

"You call this a kitchen?" He took his finger and ran it along the top edge of the cupboard, retrieving it covered with dust. "You have failed inspection. I'm demoting you to the rank of private."

"Private!" I said. "I should be the captain and you should be private."

"Gross insubordination; you'll face a court-martial for this. I'll have you thrown out of the army."

"I certainly hope so."

Taking care of our farm on even a limited basis was plenty of work. Without a tractor we couldn't work the fields, but we did try to take care of the garden we had started shortly after the summer began. And Rosie had to be milked whether we were thirsty for milk or not. Bret and I teamed together on the chores, working hard to finish by lunch. This freed the afternoon for pure play. We reinvented tag a thousand times. There was backwards tag where you had to run backwards, and blindfolded tag that really didn't work unless you cheated. But my favorite had to be tube tag. We took giant spare inner tubes from the tractor, pumped them up with air and put them around our waists. Then we bumpered and bumped like cars in a carnival midway.

In the evening, we played marathons of Monopoly and other board games. Deliriously gloating, we drove each other to the brink of bankruptcy.

"Bret you're on my hotel."

"So what?"

"So you owe me seven hundred and fifty bucks."

"Here..." He threw the money in my direction.

"You were broke the last time around the board. Where did you get seven hundred fifty dollars?"

"I saved it for an emergency."

"No you didn't," I said, "you robbed the bank."

He tried to look like he wasn't guilty, but I knew better.

"You're a cheater," I accused him. "I knew I shouldn't have let you be the banker."

I should confess that when I was the banker, I occasionally dipped into the till. I suppose that in the true spirit of capitalism, cheating at Monopoly is merely a facet of the game.

Our other main source of amusement during those nights was the radio. The local station out of Blountstown was only licensed to operate from sunup to sundown. Not that it mattered, because they didn't have much to offer except crop reports and an occasional scratchy record from the 1940s. One great thing about radio is that in the evening, the signals from all over the country start to skip and bounce from every whichawhere (that means all over). We had a small white kitchen radio, a new hi-fi model radio and an old stand up console type. Daddy and Mother loved music.

With the huge old Zenith black dialed console radio, I could turn the large brown knob on the front real slow and tune in most every big northern station, provided it was a clear night. For some reason, I could pick up Chicago's WGN more clearly than the stations a thousand miles nearer in Atlanta. Usually I preferred Jacksonville's WAPE. They called themselves "The Big Ape" and I never failed to laugh when they said it. They were on the Dumont network and had an episode of The Lone Ranger and a replay of the Jimmy Durante Show every night. Radio shows with stories like that were pretty much done with by 1963, but "The Big Ape" kept running them. Nowadays the new transistor radios don't tune in from so far away, and the big stars all have TV shows. Though for all the laughter he gave me at the time, I'd like to think that Jimmy Durante's signal is still skipping and bouncing to somewhere. "Goodnight, Mrs. Calabash wherever you are."

Chapter Seventeen

Over the course of the three weeks following, I saw in my brother Bret a slow, subtle change. He traded his goofy farmboy behavior for a pensive, almost considerate, attitude. Something inside him was different, but for the life of me I couldn't figure it out. It had been a month since he had teased me or given me an Indian burn. When we played Monopoly he never even cheated anymore. Actually, it seemed as if now he played the games only to help me occupy the evening hours.

In the South when someone stops doing all the bad things they like to do, things like drinkin' and cussin' and chasin' after women, they have a name for it. The person starts reading the Bible and going to church regularly. Generally, it's like they're a different person. What people say when this phenomenon occurs is that so an so "got religion." Usually they tell you how the subject got it, too. They'll say, "You know old Johnny Doe? Well, he got real drunk Friday night, punched a deputy sheriff in the nose, got thrown in jail for thirty days and 'got religion'." Or they might say, "You know young Janey Doe? Well, her little baby got the croup real bad and she was up all night for three nights running, with that baby in her arms chokin' and gaspin' for air. Well, that baby got better, and now Janey Doe's 'got religion'." The principal difference between men and women in this matter it seems, is that when men "get religion" it's because of something bad they've done and when women "get religion" it's because of something good that happened. It should be mentioned that when people get religion after being thrown in the pokey or having a bad thing turn out all right, it usually doesn't take. After a while, they start thinking that God probably didn't have much of a hand in their troubles or blessings after all. Before long they're back to doing whatever bad things they like to do.

Anyhow, come to find out that the reason for the change in my brother's outlook was that Bret "Got Religion." Now Bret didn't drink or cuss or do any other bad things, and no miracle happened to make everything all right for us, but somewhere out in the pasture while he was cutting hay for the cow by hand, he stood up straight and tall and the Spirit was within him.

As you might remember, when it comes to religion I'm pretty much a skeptic. So when Bret started reading from Mother's old family Bible each night, I didn't bother to join in his enthusiasm. One thing I did believe though, was that when a person finds in God solace for their pain, it's a heartless thing to discourage them.

Every day Bret would do his best to keep up with the work on the farm, fixing things and tending to the animals, while I kept the house and cooked our meals.

Each night we'd play some cards or a game of Scrabble (no more Monopoly 'cause Bret couldn't ever win since he stopped cheating). Afterward, Bret would pull what I now called "his" Bible off the shelf, choose a passage, and study it after reading it aloud.

He read to me one night,

"When I consider thy heavens, the work of thy fingers,
the moon and the stars, which thou hast ordained;
What is man, that thou art mindful of him?"

And just like Herbert Halliday had said,
"It made me stop and think." I imagined myself looking down from heaven at our little farm, and our white cracker box house. I wondered exactly what God thought of Bret and me and even Rosie.

Chapter Eighteen

One evening, a few days after that third week had passed, we finally tired of games. A cool wind blew from the north, pushing the red line on the thermometer down towards the bowl at its base. Bret brought in extra kindling, which I used to stoke the kitchen stove. We made terrible tasting hot coffee flavored milk because we had used the last of the Hershey's syrup settling an argument. We were out of Cheerios and sugar and a dozen other little things people need for comfort.

Summer was gone. Neither of us had bothered to keep track of the calendar, so we could only guess at the date. By looking at the postmark on our most recent letter from Hazel, we figured we were probably halfway through September. School had likely already started. I wondered why no one had come out to check up on us. The sun was starting to share it's time with us less and less each day. In another month, the hours of darkness would outweigh the hours of light.

That evening, while forcing down the horrible tasting coffee flavored milk I read aloud to Bret the latest letter from Aunt Hazel.

"Dear Bret and Melanie,

I haven't heard back from you with a letter, but I am assuming the two of you children are doing all right. By the time this letter gets to you, school will most likely have begun. I don't suppose it will hurt anything if you miss a week or two or three of it.

Like I told you, your cousin Lenue showed up at my door, and is stayin' here while he goes to the university. This house is only two blocks from the school and has four spare bedrooms. Lenue moving in made me realize I could rent out the other rooms to children from the college."

(Aunt Hazel always called anyone younger than 25 or so a child. She hated the word "kid" saying it was for baby goats not young people.)

"So I rented out all my rooms, and now there are young people running all over this place. And believe it or not, Lila actually has cleaning to do, as I include maid cleanup in the 40 dollars a month room rent. With so many people in the house, it seems like Cleo and Caesar are always looking out for their tails being stepped on. Right now there's no room for you two children if you decide you want to live here. But if you do decide, we can always put one of the college children down in the finished cellar. Of course these college children all like television, so Lenue and I, along with one of the roomers, went down to Sears and bought a brand new color TV. I swore I wasn't going to watch it, but the color is so pretty and that Ben Cartwright is one handsome man."

Hazel's letter went on much the same for another two pages, with her finally ending her rambling due to one of the roomers wanting to come into the house after Aunt Hazel's 11:00 p.m. curfew for borders. She signed off with a simple, "Love, Aunt Hazel."

That night, while reading through all of her letter several times and shaking our heads from side to side whenever a section of her letter confirmed our belief that dear Aunt Hazel was one crazy old lady, Bret and I talked about school and the coming of autumn weather. Our 12 turkeys (three had gone missing), 37 chickens, three geese and 4 pigs were all grown to the point where they would soon turn into breakfasts and dinners. They needed to be sold. With a nod of our heads between us, we silently decided that tomorrow there would have to be a change of seasons for ourselves as well.

I awoke the next morning surprised to be happy. Considering I had no idea how the day would turn out, I'd have thought for sure I would at least have been nervous and jittery, and cross with Bret. Don't be fooled, I was plenty scared, but adventure always suited me, regardless of my fears. Sliding my eyes around the corner, I peaked in on Bret. He was peering under his bed for what I assumed was an escaped shoe. Laid across his bed were his Easter Sunday clothes. I pulled my head back to avoid being caught as a spy.

Upon my cedar hope chest was the white and blue Easter Sunday dress I had chosen the night before. Daddy's eyes always seemed a little glassy when he saw me in this outfit. I put myself together. Sitting at my little-girl-sized vanity, I brushed my hair a hundred strokes, till it fell soft and shining onto my shoulders. Aunt Hazel had given me a tiny bottle of real perfume two birthdays before, which I opened and splashed on far too much of. I choked and fanned the air with my hand. I tried to use a small tube of lipstick I had, but my hand shook too much to let me. I slid my feet into the pair of patent leather black pumps that had such a short heel that Mother and Daddy had finally relented and consented to buy them. Snatching my purse from the edge of my bed, I wobbled on the heels into the kitchen.

Bret stood at the window, his eyes scanning the pasture. He looked fine, and maybe even a little taller than usual. He was all decked out in his dark navy suit and tie. Hearing me clump into the room, he turned away from his dreams

After a summer of seeing me chasing around in shorts and shirts, I think Bret was truly surprised by my entrance. I would swear his eyes were a little bit glassy when he first turned to face me.

"You look great, Melanie."

"Thank you, sir." I held out the edges of my skirt, pretending a curtsy.

"Are you ready?" he asked.

"More or less," I said.

Bret locked all the doors and windows while I marched out front and waited under the trees. When he joined me, he was carrying a small suitcase packed with a change of clothes for each of us.

We knew we couldn't stay on the farm alone any longer. Besides the fact that we were supposed to be in school, we were also well aware that it took money, supplies and tons of work to live on and run our farm. Crops have to be planted, grown, harvested and sold. We were not near grown up enough to take all of this on.

We walked past our property's line of trees, and the morning sun found a soft place to rest on our shoulders. A slight cool breeze, still damp from the early fog, lifted the weight from our steps. We moved briskly, never once looking back. Two miles of dusty road rolled out before us, with six miles of highway after to walk, until we would reach the center of town. My shiny black shoes fought the washboard clay, making me lose my footing on every third or fourth step.

Every time I stumbled, Bret placed his arm across my back to help me keep my balance. We were, as we always were, brother and sister and friends.

Bret and I didn't have any firm plans as to what we would do when we got to town. We did know that Rosie couldn't milk herself and that hawks would soon be after all our chickens. Bret figured the people from 4-H would know what to do with the animals. We were carrying one change of clothes and $87.00 from the cookie tin. We would walk into town, get something to eat at the Cozy Café and figure it out from there.

Epilogue

It has been nine years almost to the day since we walked away from the farm. In all of that time, never once have Bret and I discussed between us Mother and Daddy's passing away. I suppose the experiences of that summer were the words we never shared.

When we arrived in town that day, everyone was surprised to learn that Aunt Hazel had left us and we had cared for ourselves throughout the summer. After hearing our story of how we got by just fine, they finally stopped looking at us like we were the two poor orphaned Fowler children.

Even though I had sworn an oath to myself that I would never set foot inside the red brick Baptist church again, I sort of had to. You see, after we walked into town and everyone couldn't decide what to do with us, Pastor Jim and his wife took us into their home and raised us, sharing their way of life. For Bret, who had recently gotten a hold of religion, this was a perfect comfort. Myself, sometimes I had trouble following their strict Southern Baptist rules, such as no going to dances, or playing the Beatles on the radio.

Regardless of the stiffness of their faith, they gave me their love in such a way as I never once was forced to be anyone other than myself, Melanie Anne Fowler.

I'm in college now, starting my second year of school in Tallahassee. I stay with Aunt Hazel, who's now seventy-two, and still healthy as a horse. A salesman at Sears showed her a new k id of oven that uses radar to cook a whole baked potat in just three minutes. So now we eat baked potatoes   th Velveeta cheese melted into them almost every ni   t, while watching reruns of Bonanza.

So much of t' t summer follows me.

Somewhere long those eight miles that Bret and I walked into   wn, or perhaps somewhere between then and now i ime, I stumbled upon a relationship with God I'm rly sure I can live with. I can now say for certain t t I believe there is a God, and I know that He (or She is looking out for me.

A fe ears after the accident, I was baptized by Pastor Jim.   seemed so worried that I might die without being sav that I consented, if only because I knew it would se s mind at ease. It seemed a simple request to fulfill, s ng as he took us into his home and loved us. But in my art of hearts, whatever true faith in and understanding God that I have, came to me from mulling over the events of that last summer on the farm.

I remember brightly the laughter we found after falling into the green pond, and how desperately Bret and I had needed to laugh. I can still see my reflection, swamp moose antlers and all, bouncing off the still surface of the water. I fondly remember walking back to the house, our clothes soaking wet, our faces covered with warm happy tears.

So often I've thought of old man Fogarty, expending his last available effort to straighten the edge of that door, then waiting at rest patiently for a cool wind he trusted would come and restore him.

The belief I have drawn from these and similar moments my life has encountered is that when spirits are low or defeated, you may always depend on God to send you laughter. When the heat of life's battle has worn you down to the barest thread of existence, God will always send a breeze.

--->

P.S. Bret is getting married! He and Laura Lightsey, a girl he met at one of Pastor Jim's revivals, are getting hitched next April. Meanwhile, they spend their weekends out on the farm, fixing things up, slowly erasing nine years of neglect. They hope to make the place livable, just in time for their honeymoon.

P.P.S. They even plan to fix the tractor.